get Him out

Nigel White

A Soldier ... a Doctor ... a Linguist ... an Empath.

John Forbes, and Peter White have assembled a team of specialists. They are going to send their team back two thousand years .... to rescue the most famous man who ever lived.

They are going to rescue Jesus of Nazareth from the crucifixion.

But there are implications ..... can the team achieve their objective, without altering the course of human history .... and what will they learn about themselves, on their journey to the foot of the cross !

To JIMMY
BEST WISHES
Nigel White

ISBN 978-1-9164982-1-1

First published in Great Britain: April 2017
by www.sugarcubepublishing.co.uk
This second (revised) edition published February 2019.

Cover photography by: Julia Mills www.juliamills.com

Illustrated by: Sue Hofman www.suehofman.com

Printed and Bound in Great Britain by
Sarsen Press, 22 Hyde Street, Winchester, Hampshire SO23 7DR

By the same author: " **. . . . watching people cry** " Published April 2018

Thank You

I want to thank Tony for his endless patience ....

I want to thank Barbara for being at home one afternoon ....
when she so easily could have been out.

I want to thank Sue .... because her sidelights failed, the night
I tried to walk away.

And I want to thank Julia .... because she knows how much of this is true
.... and Julia isn't telling ....

DEDICATION

There's a place I went to, for the first time, when I was thirteen years old.

I saw what was done there .... but I wouldn't accept that it was done for me.

Some 45 years later, my cherished friend, Pastor Abigail Oddoye, offered to take me there again. It was late one evening .... in a quiet corner of The Destiny Centre Church, in Southampton.

We went there together .... and this time .... I accepted.

I have decided to go back to that place a third time .... but before I go .... I dedicate this book to Pastor Abigail Oddoye.

FOREWORD

This book has upset many people .... and I accept that I have lost some of my friends because of it.

But I didn't write this book to make friends.

This book pays tribute to a very brave young man.

It is my personal tribute to Jesus of Nazareth.

Nigel White
March 2017

"What is Truth?"

Pontius Pilate

"Marje – it takes two people to lie. One person to lie, and the other person to listen to them."

Homer Simpson

PROLOGUE

Julie and I were sitting in Costa. We were half way down a couple of Mochas. I prefer Cappuccino, but Julie had insisted that I try something different. It was good .... but not good enough to lure me from my Cappuccinos.

Julie pulled a Bible from her bag.

"Nigel", she said. "I've been reading the four Gospels again. Can I ask you a question .... well two questions actually".

I smiled at her.

"Go on then", I said.

"When the Disciples went to the Garden of Gethsemane with Jesus .... did they know He was going to be arrested".

"That's an interesting question Julie", I said. "Have you a reason for asking".

"Well", she said. "If they did know .... then I'm amazed that they were relaxed enough to be able to fall asleep".

I smiled at her.

"Well done", I said.

Julie looked puzzled.

"They didn't "fall asleep", I said. "Jesus drugged them".

"What .... !!!", she said.

"Ok", I said. "That's shocked you .... but just think about it for a moment. Jesus has eleven fit healthy young men on His team. What do you think those young men would be most likely to do, when the arrest starts to happen".

"They would try to protect Jesus", she said. "Perhaps put up a fight".

"Exactly", I said. "And against professional soldiers, some of them will be injured .... perhaps even killed".

"So Jesus drugged them .... to protect them", she said thoughtfully.

"A very brave, and unselfish act", I said.

"And by doing that", said Julie, ".... he lost their company and support, just when He would have needed it most of all".

I nodded.

"I think there are three reasons why He drugged His Disciples", I said. He wanted to protect them from harm. He wanted His arrest to go as peacefully as possible. And finally .... and most importantly .... He needed His Disciples fit and healthy, to continue His Ministry, when He had gone".

"But how did He manage to drug them all", she said.

I sighed.

"Julie", I said. "Think your way through the events at The Last Supper. Now is there anything Jesus did, that would have made it possible for Him to administer a soporific drug to the Disciples".

Julie closed her eyes. I could see her thinking her way through The Last Supper ....

Suddenly her eyes shot open.

"Oh My God", she said. "It's so obvious .... and yet I never saw it before ....".

I shrugged .... and smiled.

*   *   *

I went for another Mocha .... and a Cappuccino for myself.

Julie took her cup thoughtfully.

"So what was the other question", I asked her.

"Transubstantiation", she said. "What is it. I can't find any mention of it in the Bible".

I shook my head.

"You won't", I said

I thought for a moment .... and flipped open my Tablet.

"I've got a piece on the subject in my document files", I said. " Just bear with me for a moment".

I opened my files, and scrolled ....

"Got it", I said.

I passed the Tablet to her ....

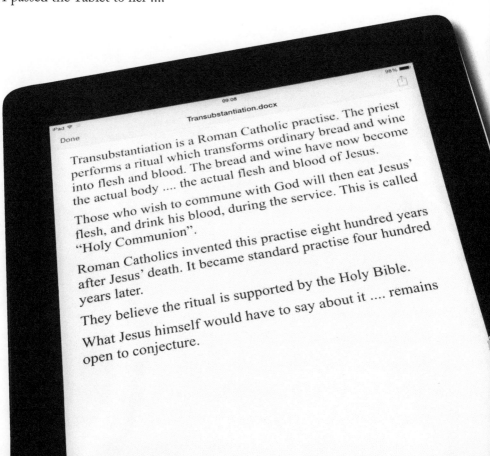

Transubstantiation.docx

Transubstantiation is a Roman Catholic practise. The priest performs a ritual which transforms ordinary bread and wine into flesh and blood. The bread and wine have now become the actual body .... the actual flesh and blood of Jesus.

Those who wish to commune with God will then eat Jesus' flesh, and drink his blood, during the service. This is called "Holy Communion".

Roman Catholics invented this practise eight hundred years after Jesus' death. It became standard practise four hundred years later.

They believe the ritual is supported by the Holy Bible.

What Jesus himself would have to say about it .... remains open to conjecture.

ONE

I was thinking about Greece .... about the Greek Islands .... about Mediterranean sun .... warm evenings .... dinner outside .... chirping crickets. I was thinking about how nice it is .... just to be warm.

The heater in the truck cab was doing what it should .... but outside .... I knew the cold was waiting for me.

I hate the cold.

There is no nicer place to be than my home in Southern England .... in the spring and summer .... perhaps even in the early Autumn.

But in the dull grey light .... the cold damp chill .... of a February afternoon .... I was thinking about Greece.

I was thinking about being warm.

I eased the truck into it's parking space at the lower end of our premises. The garden end. Yes .... it was warm in the cab .... but as I climbed down, the chilled damp air found me quickly enough. It seemed to soak through my jacket, as I reached up for my briefcase, and tucked it under my arm. I closed the cab door, and locked it. The engine would begin to cool. I was tired. It would be nice not to have to take the truck out again that day.

But money is money .... and if there's a job .... you go and do it.

I walked the length of the garden, past the apple trees, past the pond on the left, and then past the big trailer caravan on the right. I would light the stove in the trailer later .... I love a warm bedroom .... but for now .... I headed for the front door of the cottage.

* * *

As I reached the front door .... I saw the car standing in the yard. A bronze grey Toyota. New registration, and with rear screen blinds drawn down. Unusual to see rear screen blinds in Britain.

I put my briefcase in the porch, and walked towards the car. The driver's

11

door opened. The man who climbed out smiled at me. He was in his forties .... smartly dressed .... clean shaven.

"Good afternoon Mr White", he called. "It's good to see you".

He reached back into the car, and pulled out an attache case. I saw him speaking .... to somebody in the car. The near side door opened. The passenger was a little younger. He produced a similar attache case, and they came around the car towards me.

The driver smiled

"Well .... good afternoon again", he said. "I'm John Forbes".

He held out his hand.

"And this is Peter White. But don't worry .... we aren't Inland Revenue, or Environment Agency, or Jehova's Witnesses".

I laughed.

"Oh", I said. "I've had some really lively discussions with the Jehova's Witnesses".

"We know you have", said John, the driver.

"You do", I said. "How".

"Later", he laughed. "We've come to ask you to do a job for us".

"A recovery job", I said.

"Yes", he said. "A recovery job".

"Well that's what we do", I said.

"And for a long time", he added. "Twenty nine years I believe".

That surprised me .... I looked at them more closely. No .... I really didn't recognise either of them .... but they seemed to know me. I was curious .... very curious.

"It's too cold out here", I said. "Let's go in and get some tea going ....

assuming you have enough time".

"Oh .... we're good for time", said the driver. "No hurry at all. We need to explain the job to you. It's not straight forward".

I turned back towards the cottage. But as I turned, I thought I saw one of the rear sunshades in the Toyota move just a fraction.

"If you've got somebody with you", I said, "they can join us in the warm".

"We've got two people actually", said the driver, "But they'll be happy to wait until we've talked through the job".

"Ok", I said, "If you're sure".

"We're sure, Nigel", said the driver, "but thank you for offering".

I unlocked the front door, and they followed me in. I went straight to the wood burner, opened the doors, stirred the fire, and added more logs.

"A real wood fire", said the passenger.

I straightened, and turned to look at my guests. They were smartly dressed .... but in a friendly way. Checked shirts rather than plain. Collars open. Smart casual .... very smart casual.

I offered them seats at the table, and went through to the kitchen. I filled the kettle, and switched it on.

"Tea, or coffee", I asked.

They both said tea, so I reached down the big tea pot. A nice piece of studio pottery, I usually keep for dinner guests.

I went back to them .... while the kettle boiled.

"So .... Peter", I said. "Are we related in any way".

"No", he said, "No relation as far as we know".

"But .... if we were related ....".

He smiled at me.

"Yes", he said, "We would know".

I went back to the kitchen, made the tea, and came back with milk, and cups, and the tea pot, all on a tray.

"Ok", I said, "We usually just get a phone call to organise a recovery job .... not a visit from two smartly dressed men, with briefcases, in a brand new car, with two mystery passengers".

They smiled.

"Sugar anybody", I asked

"No sugar", they said.

We sat down, with our mugs of tea, and I looked at them carefully.

"I have a feeling that I'm going to hear something unusual", I said.

They glanced at each other....

"So what sort of vehicle is it that you want me to recover", I asked.

They glanced at each other again, and then, as though by pre- arranged consent, Peter started.

"Nigel", he said, "It's not a vehicle that we want you to recover for us".

"It's not a vehicle". I was puzzled. "What is it then".

"It's a person".

"A person", I said.

I began to feel rather uneasy.

"It's not a dead person, I hope".

Peter held up a hand.

"No", he said, smiling. "It's not a dead person".

I was relieved.

"I've never been asked to recover a person", I said. "Well .... only if they're with a car thats broken down".

"We realise that .... but we hope that you might agree to help us with this job", said John.

"Can I ask who it is", I said.

There was a long pause.

"You can ask", said John.

There was another pause.

I looked at them.

"So who is it", I said.

"It's Jesus of Nazareth", said John.

It would be melo-dramatic to tell you that my jaw dropped .... but you get the picture. I looked very closely at their faces .... they were serious.

"Ah", I said, suddenly seeing the light. "You mean an actor, from a film".

"No", said John, " Not an actor. We want you to recover Jesus of Nazareth".

At this point, I took a very deep breath and exhaled slowly. I took a sip of tea .... and decided biscuits were in order. I fetched a new packet from the kitchen, opened them, and offered them to my guests. They each took a biscuit, and continued to watch me closely. Neither spoke. They were waiting.

We were into crazy territory ....

"You said it was a living person", I said.

"Nigel", said Peter. "Is Jesus of Nazareth dead".

I closed my eyes.

"No", I said, "Jesus of Nazareth is not dead".

I caught a glance between them. I realised that they had been pretending to be relaxed. But now they sat back in their chairs, and sipped their tea .... and took a biscuit each.

I kept my eyes closed while I thought. I had two ways forward from here. I could tell them that I considered jokes about Jesus to be in very poor taste, and ask them to leave. Or I could be very cautious .... and give them a chance to explain themselves.

"Please don't ask us to leave, Nigel", said Peter. "At least, give us a chance to explain".

I opened my eyes, and sat there looking from one to the other.

They looked at me. They held their composure .... and they waited.

I took a deep breath.

"I don't know who you are", I said, "Or where you are from. But I have to assume, unless you are both completely insane, that a little matter of three thousand five hundred miles .... let alone the even more difficult issue of nearly two thousand years .... are not obstacles to your proposal. And if those two issues really are not a problem .... then that must surely mean that there has been a very important scientific development .... and a very secret developement at that".

"There has been a developement", said Peter. "And yes .... a very secret one".

I looked at them closely again.

"It isn't easy to lie to me", I said. "Not easy at all. There are reasons for that".

"We know", said Peter. "That's why we're here".

"Nigel", said John, "Before we go any further, there is somebody we would like you to meet".

"The inventor of time travel", I asked.

"No", said John, "Not an inventor".

He motioned to Peter........

"If you'll excuse me for a moment..........", Peter said.

He went out through the front door, closing it carefully behind him. I went to the fire, and added more logs. I turned and looked up at John.

"Why me", I asked.

John looked at me long and thoughtfully.

"Do you really need me to answer that question Nigel", he said quietly.

I closed my eyes again.

"No", I said. "I know .... but I really don't understand how you know".

* * *

There was a slight knock at the door. John went to open it, and then stood aside, as the door opened from outside. A young woman came into the room. Short dark hair, in her mid twenties, knee length skirt, subtle, but expensive blouse, and jacket, with a beautiful orange scarf.

John smiled at her.

"Nigel .... I would like you to meet Miss Julie Parker-Smith. Julie is a professor of languages at Cambridge University".

I offered my hand, and she took it carefully, and held it for a moment.

"Let me guess", I said. "You specialise in ancient languages of the Eastern Mediterranean .... and you are really good at Aramaic".

She laughed. A really nice girl, I thought.

"Nigel", she said, "I'm so pleased to meet you at last".

"At last", I said. "I'm feeling I'm the only one not in the loop here".

Then she stepped closer, and put her arms around me, and pressed her hair against the side of my face. Her perfume gave me an emotional jolt.

"Estee Lauder "White Linen", I said. "And I'm guessing you didn't choose that paricular perfume by accident".

"No", she said quietly, "Not by accident".

Then she stepped back a little, and I saw the person who had entered the room behind her.

It was another young woman. Although her head was bowed, and carefully covered with a scarf, I caught a glimpse of olive skin and dark lashes. Julie raised her hand to her cheek. The young woman seemed to accept this as a signal that all was well. She raised her own hands and removed her scarf.

Now up to this moment .... right up to this exact moment .... I had listened to what they told me with a sense of disbelief, perhaps even with a sense of humour.

And then I looked at this young woman. And I knew immediately that she wasn't from our time .... or our place.

My brother always says that if you look at Victorian photographs, you know the people portrayed in them are not from our world. His theory is that a face contains what you know. And those ladies and gentlemen, gazing at us from pictures taken one hundred years ago .... they just didn't have our knowledge. My brother doesn't mean academic knowledge. He means, "what you know".

"However hard you try", he says, "and however good the makeup artist is, you cannot take modern people and fake a Victorian photograph. One look at the faces, and you can see that the people are modern. They just know far too much".

So I looked at this young woman .... and that's when everything changed .... and the situation became very real. Very real indeed.

And yes .... I admit it. I fell in love with Her at that moment. Of course I did. But not in the normal way. If there is a normal way to fall in love.

I was absolutely fascinated by her. Shall I describe her.

Young. Seventeen .... perhaps eighteen. Calm. Thoughtful. Serene. She was wearing a grey wool cloth dress. Three quarter length. The most perfect olive skin. Dark eyes. Dark lashes. Tumbling dark curls.

She raised her head and looked steadily into my eyes. The others in the room seemed to sense something special was happening. They stood and waited..

"Nigel", said Peter. "May I present.....".

And I knew what he was going to say. And I didn't want him to say it. Because once it was said .... I was committed.

I couldn't look at her any more. I gently dropped to my knees in front of her, and took her right hand, and pressed it to my forehead.

"Nigel", said Peter, "May I present to you Mary of Magdala .... Mary Magdalene".

I kept perfectly still, her hand against my forehead. She pressed her other hand to my right cheek, and spoke .... just a few words.

Julie interpreted.

"She asks why you kneel to her", Julie said.

"Then ask her if I may rise", I said.

Julie spoke.

The Magdalene put her fingers beneath my chin, and lifted me. I stood before her again, and she took my hands in hers, and spoke for the second time.

"She bids that the Blessing of God be upon you", Julie said.

"The Hebrew God whose Ark this is", I said.

"Yes", said Julie, "The Hebrew God whose Ark this is".

So we stood holding hands .... and we looked at each other.

And then it simply became too much. I went and stood facing the fire, and I looked into the flames.

They let me alone.

Eventually the Magdalene came and placed her hand on my shoulder. She spoke again.

"She asks if you will help us", Julie said.

I found that tears didn't matter. I turned towards my guests, straightened, and looked at Mary of Magdala.

"Yes", I said, "I will help you".

TWO

However much you have been shocked, or surprised .... however emotional you have become .... there comes a time when you have to get to grips with what has happened. You must take a moment .... to assess.

So I drew out two more chairs, saw all my guests seated, and went back to the kitchen to organise fresh tea. And to get a great many questions into some sort of order.

I found two more mugs.

"Julie", I said, "Will Mary......................................".

I stopped.

"Look", I said, "I'm sorry .... I can't just call her Mary. This is Jesus' girlfriend in my living room. This is completely crazy. I've got Jesus' girlfriend sitting in my living room .... and I'm calling her Mary .... like this is just an every day occurrence".

Julie laughed. She turned to Mary, and the two girls conversed. Mary blushed as the situation was explained to her. The two of them seemed to reach a conclusion they were both happy with, and Mary glanced up at me, and smiled.

"I have asked if you can call her Magdalena", Julie said to me. "Mary is happy with that .... I've tried to explain to her that you feel a need to show her very special respect, but she is not sure why".

I went to the Magdalena.

"Magdalena", I said "It is very very special for me .... to have this opportunity to meet you".

Julie translated

The Magdalena smiled at me. She spoke again to Julie. The two girls laughed together. I raised my eyebrows at Julie.

"Sorry Nigel", said Julie, "I'm not going to translate everything .... that was definitely girl talk".

Peter coughed discretely.

"Nigel", he said, "You must have questions for us".

"Oh yes", I said, "I've got questions .... lots and lots of questions for you".

"Before we start", said John, "It will be best if Julie keeps the Magdalena informed of our conversation .... so we might need short breaks for Julie to keep up".

"Yes", I said, "I understand that .... thats fine".

"Ok", said John, "Where do you want to start".

I didn't reply immediately. I poured four mugs of tea. To my surprise the Magdalena took hers readily when Julie passed it to her. So Mary Magdalene sat, and sipped tea, in my living room.

I made an assessment of the situation. The proposal was crazy. It had to be crazy. But if this really was Mary Magdalene sitting here .... and I knew in my heart that it was .... then everything else they had told me had to be at least plausible.

"Ok", I said. "I understand that this is the real Mary Magdalene from first century Nazareth".

"Well .... from Magdala, to be stictly accurate", said Peter.

"Ok", I said."But if this lady is here, I assume She is not in Magdala at the moment .... or two thousand years ago".

"No", said Peter, "She is here .... not there".

"Which leads to the first question .... and it's an important question. At what point in "the story" .... the sequence of events .... have you lifted Her from. For instance .... has Her relationship with Jesus started yet".

"Yes", said Peter, "Her relationship with Jesus is well established".

Suddenly there were a number of questions I wanted to ask.

"You know what I'm longing to ask", I said.

"No", said John, "She definitely wasn't .... and never was".

"Ah", I said, smiling, "I thought not".

"And now you actually know", said John.

The possibilities opened up before me.

"But remember", said Peter, quickly, "Mary .... sorry .... the Magdalena .... only knows the story up to the point where we lifted her from. That's why She was puzzled by your reverence".

I thought about that for a moment.

"Right", I said. "I think I need to know how close things are to the end game .... meaning the crucifixion .... at the moment you brought the Magdalena out. Are we months away, or weeks away .... or just days away".

"Julie fetched The Magdalena for us two days after Jesus raised her brother Lazarus from the dead", said John.

"So The Magdalena, and Lazarus, really are brother and sister.... and Martha is sister to them", I said.

"Yes", said Peter. "In fact .... it is remarkable how acurate the accounts in the New Testament are when you come to details".

I thought about that.

"Look", I said."I am obviously fascinated to know how all this is possible .... but I have a feeling that the science of it is going to be way beyond me. So, for the moment, I'll accept your word that it is possible to move through time".

"Actually", said John, "the science of it is really amazingly simple, and we can explain the basic ideas that make it workable".

"But, Ok, accepting that it is possible", I said, "Why do you need me. Why can't you lift Jesus out of that world before He's in real danger. Before the arrest".

"I'm afraid", said John, "that it is not quite that simple .... not in the case of Jesus".

"I had a feeling it wouldn't be", I said.

"By the way", I added. "Is Jesus really the Son of God".

John and Peter both laughed.

"We don't know that", said John. "But He is very convincing in the role. Raising Lazarus from the dead is quite an act".

There was a long pause, broken only by the musical sound of Julie speaking to the Magdalena in Aramaic. She caught up.

The girls looked to us. I was sitting there shaking my head.

"This is a lot to get my head around", I said. "You've all had some time to get used to the idea. How long has The Magdalena been here".

"Two months", said John.

"And can you put her back at the same moment in time you took her from", I asked.

"Yes", said John, "We can really only put her back in the exact moment we took her from, because we don't understand the consequences of doing anything else".

"I see", I said. "That makes sense .... if anything does about this".

"I think I should stop asking questions", I said, and we should move on to you telling me what you have in the way of a plan. There is a plan I hope".

"Yes", said John, "There is a plan".

"Nigel", said Peter. "It might be good to take a break at this point. Mary .... sorry ... The Magdalena .... tires easily, and our Doctor checks her over every twelve hours. What I suggest is that we return to our Hotel for now, and either John, or myself, will collect you at say 7.30, and you can join us for dinner. Would that be Ok with you".

"Any dinner I don't have to cook is definitely Ok with me", I said.

"Dinner at eight then", said John. They stood to leave.

The Magdalena took Julie's hand, and reached for mine. John and Peter seemed familiar with the action. They completed the circle.

The Magdalena spoke for a few moments.

"She asks for Gods Blessing .... that we shall travel safely and meet again soon", Julie said.

We said "Amen".

26

THREE

By the time I'd seen my guests back to their car, and seen them safely out onto the road, it was nearly five thirty in the afternoon. It was now fully dark, and the air felt horribly damp and cold.

I had a couple of hours before the car would collect me for dinner at the hotel.

I went back indoors, tended the fire, and sat down to think. The last hour and a half had been surreal. But I only had to remember my first sight of the Magdalena's face to know that it was all real enough. This young woman just wasn't from our time. She was, in every way, part of the first century Holy Land.

I considered my future.

If Julie really had gone back in time, to fetch the Magdalena .... were they intending to send me back to recover Jesus of Nazareth. And if they were .... at what point in the story would we spirit Him away. And what would the consequences of that action be on history. The more I thought about it, the more I began to see that there could only be one tiny window of opportunity, if we were going to preserve history . But that was a very big if.

Unless John, Peter, or Julie, or even the Magdalena, had a plan that I hadn't thought of .... this particular recovery job might prove to be extremely dangerous.

I went to the bathroom, switched on the electric heater, and the shower, and left things to warm up.

Back in the living room I had a strong desire for a glass of wine, but I'd given up alcohol two years ago, and dealing with these short lived cravings was no longer the problem it had been. I dismissed the idea, and found a can of Coke in the fridge. I wondered what I would drink in first century Jerusalem. Wine was safer than water. I certainly did not want Cholera.

Perhaps they wouldn't need me to go back.

I took a while over the shower, then pondered on what to wear .... and ended up in my smartest jeans, a soft linen red checked shirt, and lace up black shoes. Before I dressed, I looked thoughtfully at the cross on it's chain around my neck. For the Magdalena .... the cross hadn't happened yet. I tucked it safely inside my shirt .... and decided to wear a tie. After all .... it was a chilly evening.

It was awe inspiring to remember that at the moment they recovered the Magdalena, the events that would change the world forever, simply hadn't happened yet.

Had they told Her what was to come.

I didn't know.

For the next three quarters of an hour, I sat and read Marks Gospel, and I paused as I came to 15:24.

"And when they had crucified Him, they parted his garments, casting lots amongst them, what every man should take".

And then, as always, 15:25, the single line that cuts right into your soul. The single line that tells you Mark was right there, on the spot, watching it happen.

"And it was the third hour.... and they crucified Him".

Almost two thousand years. But in that simple repetition .... Mark contrives to expresses the horror of what he has seen. All his shock, and despair, and grief, in one single line.

Yes. Mark had been there. He had witnessed the crucifixion.

I had often wondered about his relationship to Jesus. And now I could find out. I could ask the Magdalena.

*　*　*

A red glow appeared in the frosted glass of the front door, and I knew my lift had arrived. I checked to see everything was safe in the kitchen, and opened the front door just as Peter was about to knock.

"I'm ready", I said.

"Nigel", said Peter, "It would be easier for us if you could stay overnight. Would that be a problem".

That took me by surprise, but I said I was Ok with it, and went off to collect my small travel bag. I found a change of clothes, and a tooth brush. Don't forget your tooth brush!

I returned to Peter in the living room.

"That's great", he said, "Incidentally .... from this point on you are on £100 per day expenses, until you decide to leave us. You can opt out at any time .... but we don't think you will".

"£100 per day", I repeated. "I'm OK with that".

"And there will be a lump sum at the end of things as a thankyou", added Peter., "Or some sort of pension, depending on how things pan out. In short .... we will look after you from here on, if you can help us".

"Well", I said, "Lets hear the plan, and then I'll know how I feel about things".

"How do you feel about things so far", said Peter.

"Oh", I said, "Fairly routine sort of a day so far. Couple of recovery jobs in the morning. Mary Magdalene round for afternoon tea. And then dinner out .... talking over plans to rescue The Messiah. Everyday story of country folk really".

Peter laughed.

"Are you ready", he said.

I glanced around, went to the stove, and closed it up tight.

"Let's go", I said.

We went out, and I locked up behind us.

The Toyota was warm, very warm. I guessed that the Magdalena would be finding Britain in January, a very cold place to be.

"So how far are we going", I asked.

"Only about 5 miles", said Peter. "We're staying at a Premier Travel Inn".

I laughed. Peter glanced at me.

"Sorry", I said. "It's just the thought of Mary Magdalene staying at a Premier Travel Inn .... Sorry".

"It's Ok", said Peter. "I appreciate that things must seem a bit surreal to you .... but you'll understand when we get there".

*   *   *

The journey took ten minutes, and sure enough, we parked outside our local Travel Inn. We didn't, however go to the front door, and the reception. Peter led me round to the side of the building, and stopped at a plain brown door, with a key pad on the wall. He punched in a code, opened the door for me, and followed me into a very smart hall way.

"There's an appartment on the top floor", said Peter, "that was built for the area manager. It's very comfortable, all facilities. We've rented it for the duration".

We went to a set of doors. Peter pressed buttons, the doors opened, and a lift appeared.

"Going up", said Peter.

The Hotel only had four floors, so it was quick.

We stepped out into another hall way. It was very warm. Peter led me to what was obviously the entrance door to the apartment. He knocked, opened the door, and beckoned me in. John and Julie stood up to meet me. We were in a very nicely decorated lounge, and from it's size, I guessed this appartment must occupy virtually the entire top floor of the Hotel.

I shook hands with them again .... Julie first.

"Premier's area manager does well for himself", I said.

John laughed.

"It certainly suits us at the moment", he said.

I stood and looked round. Although it was very nicely decorated and furnished .... it was still a hotel in every way. No personal touches.

"Take a seat", said John, beckoning me to a Sofa. "The Magdalena is in her room with the Doctor, at the moment .... but they won't be much longer".

"We couldn't quarantine her", said Julie, so the Doctor checks her over every twelve hours. No problems so far though, which is a relief".

"She certainly appears very healthy to me", I said. "Have you given her any innoculations".

"No, we haven't", said Julie. "When we were planning this, there was an enormous amount of discussion about immunisation .... but it was decided it was too risky. If, after a while, the doctor assures us that the experience has not effected her .... then we might look at it again. But her own people have plenty of hygiene rules in place, and we have observed that she is just as careful here as she is at home. She loves our modern soaps and shampoos".

At this moment the door opened, and a very efficient looking lady in her forties came into the room.

I stood up, as did Peter, and John.

"Nigel", said John, "This is Doctor Verena Samuels. She is keeping a very careful eye on the Magdalena .... in fact they have a chat every twelve hours or so".

I shook her hand.

"Doctor Samuels .... I'm pleased to meet you", I said. "And is the Magdalena in good health".

"The Magdalena is in perfect health, I'm pleased to tell you", said the Doctor.

I noticed her looking at me carefully .... as though assessing me for the project.

"I'm pleased to meet you, at last", she said. "I've booked you for an appointment in my surgery at 9.30 tomorrow morning. I'm right up to date with your medical records, but I'd like to check you over, and generally have a chat. Are you comfortable with a female Doctor or.....".

"I'm perfectly comfortable with a female Doctor", I said.

"Good", she said, "Now I had intended to join you all for dinner, but I have some matters, back at my surgery, that need my attention .... so if you'll excuse me, I'll see you at 9.30 tomorrow morning. Peter will bring you in the car, and he'll wait until we've finished".

I looked at Peter, who nodded.

Doctor Samuels wished the others a good evening, and left us .... saying that the Magdalena would join us shortly.

John, Peter, and I, resumed our seats .... only to rise almost immediately as the Magdalena came quietly into the room. She came straight to me, took my hands in hers, looked up into my eyes, and spoke to me. The language had a musical quality that I found fascinating. Her enunciation seemed clear and educated, even though I could not understand the words. I looked to Julie, who had come to stand next to her.

"The Magdalena bids you welcome", Julie said, "and she hopes that the time will soon come when she may offer you the hospitality of her Father's house. She looks forward to introducing you to her parents, and her brother Lazarus, and her sister Martha".

"Tell her .... that subject to The Lord's will .... I will look forward to those meetings with much pleasure", I said.

Julie translated. The Magdalena nodded, and went to sit on the empty sofa. Peter motioned me to join her.

She turned to Julie, and spoke for a few moments. Julie nodded and turned to me.

"The Magdalena wishes to know how old you were when you realised that you had a gift from God".

I was not expecting the question.

"Just four years old", I answered. "In fact the day I started school, which was well before I was five .... due to my having been born in May".

Julie translated, while The Magdalena listened carefully. She asked Julie a question.

"She wishes to know if you have found your gift a burden".

"No .... not a burden", I said, "because by the time I was five, I had found a way to switch it off. It was too embarassing to have the ability all the time".

Again Julie translated. Then the Magdalena stood. She motioned us to remain seated .... and came behind me as I sat. She layed a hand on my head. She spoke.

"She asks that you share with her", said Julie.

I closed my eyes .... but in my mind I opened a door that was nearly always kept closed. I felt the Magdalena's hand tense .... then relax again.

And then she sighed.

She returned to her seat, and spoke softly to Julie.

"The Magdalena says that you opened the door only a fraction", said Julie.

"I know", I said. "I find it better to go in small stages".

Julie passed this to the Magdalena, who nodded.

"She understands", Julie said. "She says trust will come with time".

* * *

There was a knock at the double doors that I guessed led to a dining room. A young man in a smart white apron over black shirt and trousers came into the room.

"Ladies and Gentlemen", he announced, "Dinner is served".

Then he smiled.

They were good words to hear. My usual afternoon snack just hadn't happened today, and biscuits only keep you going for so long.

We seated ourselves at the dining table. The room was pleasantly warm, and the chairs were very comfortable. I found myself next to The Magdalena, with Julie seated at her right hand. Opposite me I had John. Peter sat opposite Julie.

"I think we're having roast lamb with seared mediterranean vegetables", Peter said, watching me closely.

I narrowed my eyes at him.

"Is there anything about me that you don't know", I asked.

"Nothing", said Peter.

"Left or right", I asked.

"Left", said Peter.

"And am I........".

"No", said Peter, "but it looks as though you are".

Julie looked at me, and raised her eyebrows.

"Julie", I said "That was boy talk .... please do not translate".

"I wouldn't dream of giving your secrets away", she said.

"Secrets", I said, "What possible secrets could I have from you all".

"Ok", I said, "Seriously now .... how did you come to find me".

"We thought you would ask that sooner or later", said John.

"I'm asking sooner", I said.

The soup arrived. The young waiter was swift and very adept. The bowls were small but the tomato soup was very much the genuine home made article.

I was startled that the Magdalena ate so swiftly. Instead of the buttered bread rolls that John, Peter, Julie, and I had, she dipped her bread into a small bowl of olive oil. I noticed that she seemed to hold her spoon a little awkwardly .... and I wondered if she would be more at ease drinking from the bowl. But for all her awkwardness, she finished her soup first, and spoke to Julie.

"The Magdalena asks that she be allowed to place a blessing upon our main course", Julie told us.

We smiled, and nodded our assent.

Our waiter removed the soup bowls, and returned with our main course already plated up. It was roast lamb .... with a side dish of mediterranean vegetables.

"We chose it just for you", said Peter.

"Lamb is a real treat for me", I said.

"For all of us", said John.

Julie motioned us to silence, and the Magdalena spoke the Grace. Her musical voice came near to a song, and I looked to Julie.

Julie sat transfixed.

I looked back to the Magdalena, who finished the Grace by passing her hand over the food.

She spoke to Julie.

"That was the original Lords Prayer", said Julie. "Jesus taught it to her two weeks ago. But it was more beautiful than I can translate for you".

I think we were all getting our heads around the fact that, for The Magdalena, The Lords Prayer, was just fourteen days old.

"I wish I could give you the real feel of that", Julie said. "Aramaic was a

35

street language. Think of a current young inner city Londoner .... and the way he would talk .... then have him invent The Lords Prayer. But Aramaic is also amazingly poetic, and Jesus knew how to use it.

But it was a street talk prayer non the less".

"Wouldn't it be fantastic if somebody found copies of the four Gospels in Aramaic", John said.

"Every modern Bible scholars dream", I said.

We began the meal in silence.

Lamb is always good, and Simon had cooked it properly. There was a fashion some years ago for serving it rare, but you just don't get the same flavour. And it always gave me indigestion.

"Nigel", said John. "You haven't asked us how we are involved in this".

"No", I said. "I really don't need to know .... it's the Magdalena that proves your story. If I was guessing I would say that one of you, or even both of you, are from the research department of a company into electronics .... and you both studied religious history at university".

John and Peter both laughed.

"You're not far off Nigel", he said.

Then he narrowed his eyes.

"Have you ....".

"No .... I haven't", I said. "That was all common sense. You have The Magdalena, and you are very obviously sufficiently funded. I'm happy".

"Yes", said Peter. "John and I were in the same sort of place as the NASA students who thought of running photographs of The Turin Shroud under the VP8 image analyser. Are you familiar with The Shroud".

I laughed.

"I am", I said. "And I'm very much looking forward to some interesting conversations with you all".

FOUR

Julie and The Magdalena left us a little before 9pm. Dessert had been banana splits .... of all things !

Julie explained to me that The Magdalena thought our ice cream was amazing .... heaven in a dish. She wouldn't consider anything else to finish a meal. Doctor Samuels had forbidden her coffee. She wanted The Magdalena to have every chance of natural sleep.

As they left the room, The Magdalena came to me, and offered her hand. I took it, and held it gently, and closed my eyes. The others fell silent. We stayed like that for perhaps a minute. Then she bent and whispered a single word in my ear. She turned, and left the room.

I looked to Julie.

She coloured.....

"I'm sorry", she said, "I didn't catch that........".

But I knew she had.

Then Julie said goodnight, and left us.

The waiter brought coffee .... two thermos insulated jugs of coffee .... another jug of milk, and sugar in sachets.

"We'll fend for ourselves now Simon", said John.

Simon nodded.

"If you want a snack later .... I've left biscuits for you all", he said.

"I'll say goodnight then gentlemen".

We wished him Good night.

We eached poured a coffee. There was a long silence.

"We'll start with a question", said John. "We have to start somewhere ....

and then we'll let things develop".

"Nigel", he said. "Do you believe Jesus of Nazareth survived the crucifixion".

This surprised me .... but it was as good a place to start as any.

"No", I said, "I do not believe He survived the crucifixion".

John and Peter glanced at each other.

"Do you have a specific reason for saying that", Peter asked.

"Yes", I said, "The spear thrust killed Him. The Roman soldiers were trained to kill with a single thrust of the spear .... the pilum. Jesus could not have survived that spear thrust".

"Now", said John. "Do you believe that there was an intention amongst various interested parties .... even a plan perhaps .... that Jesus would survive the crucifixion".

I looked at them both carefully, trying to work out where this might be heading. I sipped my coffee.

"If", I said, slowly, "If you read the four Gospels carefully, there are plenty of indications that a rescue attempt had been planned".

They nodded.

"Would you like to elaborate on that", said John.

"Ok", I said. "There are several incidents that jump out at me. First .... Jesus refusal of the pain reliever, before the nailing started. Then His reaction when the vinegar on Hissop was given to Him. Third .... the fact that His legs were not broken. Fourth .... Pontious Pilate surrendering the body to Joseph of Aramathea. In fact Pilates odd behaviour throughout the whole thing, raises questions. Then we have to wonder about the short time Jesus spent on the cross .... and we could ask more questions about the herbs that Joseph and Nicodemus carried into the tomb.........

Will that do .... because there are plenty more clues where those came from .... and they all come from the four Gospels. That is what is so totally

amazing about those four Gospels. The detail. The information is there ....
but most people ignore the detail, because they think they know the story.
They just don't bother to read the small print".

John stared long and hard at me. He looked to Peter.

"Let's take that list appart then", said Peter. "From the start. Why do you
think he refused the pain reliever".

"Same reason I don't eat breakfast before going to the Dentist", I said. "If
you book an early morning appointment, and don't eat breakfast ..... your
digestive system is bare. If you have to have a filling ..... well the cocaine hits
you hard and fast. You don't feel a thing".

"Like drinking alcohol on an empty stomach", said Peter.

"Exactly like that", I said, "And you'll remember that Jesus wouldn't drink
wine at the last supper".

"I shall not partake of the fruit of the vine, until I taste it anew in My
Father's house", said Peter, thoughtfully.

"That's it", I said, "And I suspect that he didn't eat either. He was giving
himself every chance for that "vinegar" to knock him out".

"Im sorry" said John. " But Jesus refused the pain reliever surely".

"Of course He did", I said. "That was before the crucifixion. You're
forgetting the sponge soaked in vinegar near the end. He knew that was
coming and He wanted it to hit him hard and fast.... as it did. He "died" just
after drinking from that sponge".

They looked at each other.

"His legs", asked Peter.

"It follows on quite logically", I said. "If you have a rescue plan, the last
thing you want is a Jesus who won't be able to walk for weeks, perhaps
months.

 Although it sounds barbaric, the Roman guards were often bribed to break the legs of crucifixion victims. If the crucified man cannot push upwards with his legs, he will suffocate. Hanging on just his arms, he cannot exhale. Suffocation is inevitable".

Again, they both nodded.

"Pilate's behaviour", said John.

"Well its downright odd from start to finish", I said. "The Scribes and Pharisees bring Jesus to him, when they themselves have the legal power to have Him stoned to death. But no .... they insist He is crucified .... the Roman method of execution. The problem for Pilate is that he can't find a good reason to give the death sentence. Jesus hadn't broken any Roman laws worthy of a death sentence. And yet Pilate hands Him over to be crucified. He was quite clever enough to percieve that the Temple authorities want Jesus dead .... but they want the Romans to be responsible for the execution. And yet .... he agrees to go along with it.

But .... think about this .... if Pilate knew the rescue plan was in place .... he can give the Temple what they want .... and yet Jesus will survive. I think Pilate knew exactly what was planned. If you have any doubts .... look at his reaction when Joseph of Aramathea asks for the body. Pilate can't be seen to agree too readily .... so he asks if it's possible that Jesus can have died so quickly. Remember .... He has been on the cross for six hours at the most. It normally took three days, sometimes a week, for crucifixion victims to die on the cross.

So having been assured by the Centurion that Jesus really is dead, Pilate hands over the body. Why did he do that. The coming Sabbath was a Jewish festival , it meant nothing to the Romans. Crucifixion victims were never taken down. The body was left to rot, in public, as a visible deterrent to the population. Thats why archeologist have only ever found one crucified skeleton. Normally the remains fell from the cross, and it was left to carrion and dogs to clear them up".

John and Peter sat staring at me.

Eventually Peter spoke.

"And the herbs they took into the tomb .... you mentioned those".

"Again", I said, "The detail is astonishing . An hundred pounds weight of healing herbs. Not embalming herbs. Healing herbs. They were expecting an injured Jesus .... an unconscious Jesus .... not a dead Jesus".

"But it went wrong for them", said John.

"Yes", I said. "It went wrong simply because some enthusiastic young soldier, with a new spear, is keen to show off. You can so easily see how it happened.

"Is He dead", asks the Centurion. Our young soldier looks at Jesus, and suddenly realises he can make sure of it. Totally sure....

Bang .... in goes the spear. "He's dead now Sarge", the soldier calls back to him. You can imagine that Centurion frozen to the spot. All his promotion prospects gone, in a split second".

Peter and John were transfixed. They were right there watching it .... they could see it.

Eventually John spoke.

"It's a fascinating theory Nigel", he said slowly.

I stayed silent.

"Or is it more than a theory for you", he said.

I stayed silent.

"Nigel", he said. "Is this more than a theory for you".

I stayed silent.

Then I started to cry.

Sometimes tears are not embarassing.

"Nigel .... would you prefer to call it a night", Peter asked softly.

"Yes", I said. "I'd like to call it a night".

Peter showed me to the bed room they'd prepared for me.

He drew the blinds, and then stood, seeming unsure as to whether he should leave me.

"We're here if you need us", he said. He closed the door softly behind him.

I went onto my knees at the bed.

"Awesome God", I prayed, "Not tonight .... please not tonight. But .... Awesome God. As always .... Your will .... not mine".

FIVE

Peter eased the Toyota into a parking space at the Medical Centre.

I had been woken at 7.45 with a breakfast of tea, and hot croissant, served by our waiter of the previous evening. He placed the tray on a small table inside my bedroom door, and withdrew.

I showered .... en suite is always nice when you are away from home, dressed in the change of clothes I'd brought with me, and carried my tray back through to the living room. Peter and John were at breakfast there. No sign of the girls yet.

Peter and I left at 9 o'clock. We drove for about half an hour.

He led me through the Medical Centre Reception area, down two corridors, and then knocked at a door labelled "Dr V. Samuels".

"Come in", I heard her call.

"I'll be in the car", said Peter, "Phone calls to make".

I felt quite at ease with her. The room was more sitting room than surgery, and I had to look closely before I spotted an alcove with a curtain accross it.

Doctor Samuels came to me, shook my hand ,and motioned me to a chair at her desk.

She looked long and thoughtfully at me.

"Heavy night, last night", she asked

"Yeah", I said. "You could say that".

She nodded.

"Are you alright with me going ahead", she asked.

I nodded.

"Time travel", she said.

"We had absolutely no idea what effects, physical, or physcological, it would have on the human body .... and we still don't know .... despite having Julie, and The Magdalena to observe.

To give you some idea of the problems we were expecting", she said, "the body's own clock is very important for women. I've had to pull the plug on several airline stewardess' careers. Long haul flying is the worse. Some girls, after flying long haul for six months, don't know whether they should be eating breakfast or dinner, don't know whether its summer or winter, and as for their period .... they don't know whether it should have begun last week, this week, or two weeks next Tuesday".

"I know", I said. "I knew a girl who flew long haul for BA. In the end her Doctor had to call time on it .... for just the reasons you've mentioned".

"Anyway", said Doctor Samuels, "So far our fears appear to have been unfounded. Julie and Mary have made the trip without any apparent harm .... in fact Julie has made two trips .... out and return, as you might say".

"But", she said, "and it is an important BUT, they are far younger than you are ....".

I winced.

"I know", I said. "I'd worked that out all by myself".

"The only observation I have made" she said, "is that The Magdalena seems to tire very easily. But I personally think this is simply due to her mentally having to take in so much new information and knowledge as she encounters our world. After a while she just wants to be by herself, switch off, and assimilate what she's seen, before she can cope with any more".

"How old is the Magdalena", I asked.

"I'm not totally certain" said Dr. Samuels, "but she's unlikely to be much beyond her seventeenth birthday".

I winced again. Seventeen was very young to cope with what was ahead of her.

There was a pause.

44

Doctor Samuels smiled at me. She looked to her computer screen, and then at the notes on her desk.

My medical record, I presumed.

"So lets begin properly", she said.

"I'm ready when you are", I said.

"So how are you feeling today Mr White".

I laughed.

"I'm very well thank you", I said.

"Ok", she said, "We'll start with some routine checks".

I nodded.

For the next ten minutes, we did my blood pressure, and my pulse, she listened to my lungs, stared into my eyes, stared down my throat, weighed me, and asked the normal questions about how well I slept, and about smoking and drinking. I was sure she already knew the answers to these .... that she'd asked more out of habit, than a need to know.

Eventually she sat down, made a couple of notes, and looked thoughtfully at me.

"You are good for your age", she said. "Very good in fact".

"That's good to hear", I said.

"Just a couple of things to talk about then", she said.

I nodded.

"That .... ehm .... condition you contracted. Does it trouble you much".

"Barely at all now", I said. "Initially it wasn't much fun".

"Not as much fun as ....".

"No", I said hastily.

"I am sorry", she said. "That was wrong of me".

I laughed.

"I'd have said the same thing".

"You know why it happened", she asked.

I nodded slowly.

"Yes", I said, "I understand why".

"He doesn't miss much, does He", she said.

"Are you religious, then", I asked.

"Nigel", she said "I'm like you. I don't believe in God. I know there is a God".

"Then you ....".

"Yes" she said. "Like you, I had an encounter that changed my life. It turned me "inside out and upside down". That's the phrase you use to describe what happened to you on the 24th May 2014, isn't it".

"How do you know so much about me", I said.

"That's Peter's department", she said. "Ask him".

"Now lets get to the part that really interests me. The day you started school .... and what you realised that day".

"Is this part of my examination", I asked slowly.

"No", she said. "To be honest, it's not, but its the part about you that has caused you to be here this morning, and it absolutely fascinates me".

I took a few moments to collect my thoughts.

"Ok", I said. "I have to explain that I didn't mix at all with other children until I started school. My parents kept me quite separate. That wasn't difficult because we lived down a tiny lane in a small village. I don't know why they kept me apart .... I wondered later if it was because I was born

46

before they were married. They did marry when I was about one year old .... after my Father's first wife had died. He had his first wife, and their four children, and his new girl friend, with little baby me, living in the same village".

The Doctor raised her eyebrows.

"Yes", I said, "It must have given the village ladies something to chat about in the Post Office on wet mornings".

"And the morning you started school ....".

"Well", I said. "If you don't mix with anybody else .... then you don't realise you are different. Simple as that".

"So what was this difference you suddenly became aware of", she said.

This was a difficult question. How to explain what I realised that day.

"This is difficult", I said.

"Try", she said.

"It was like they were deaf", I said. "They couldn't hear me .... and it was obvious they couldn't hear each other .... I don't mean they were physically deaf ....".

"I know you don't", she said.

"I could sort of scan them", I said, "scan their minds .... and they didn't know I was doing it. That bit was missing from them. They were sort of primitive in the sense that their minds were isolated .... the only feelings they were aware of .... were their own. And they were so selfish because of it ....".

"How about the teachers", said Dr. Samuels.

"Just the same", I said. "They didn't know I could scan them .... do you understand what I mean when I say "scan them".

"I think so", she said. "You could read their feelings and emotions".

"I could connect to their feelings, and their emotions", I said, "and they had no idea I was doing it .... and they had absolutely no way to read my feelings .... to know my emotions".

That scared me .... they could hurt me, and they wouldn't even know they were doing it".

"What did you do" she said.

"I got through the day", I said. "But I was determined never to go back. It took three people to get me out of my Mother's car every morning"

"Did you tell your Mother why", she said.

"I was about four and a half years old", I said. "I couldn't describe the situation then, like I can now".

She nodded.

"Was there nobody there for you to connect to".

"Nobody", I said. "After a while I learned to "switch off" my ability .... not completely though".

"But you still have the ability in its full sense".

"Yes", I said, "In fact .... I found out later, that the ability goes beyond our own time and place".

"Ah", she said. "Now I begin to understand".

"Why I'm here you mean".

"Yes", she said. "Has it ever scared you".

I looked long and hard at her.

Oh yes .... it had scared me .... really scared me on one occasion.

"Once .... badly", I said.

"Do you want to tell me about it", she said.

Then she seemed to think of an idea.

"Tell you what", she said, "Lets go and get a coffee at Costas. My treat".

"Will there be Lemon zesty tarts", I said.

"If you like", she said.

"Don't forget Peter", I said. "He's waiting in the car for me".

"I'll phone him", she said.

She reached for her mobile phone, and I watched her scroll for Peter's number.

"Peter", she said. "I've persuaded Nigel to go for a coffee with me. I'll bring him back to the hotel when I come to give The Magdalena her check over".

She listened for a few moments, said goodbye to Peter, and put the phone in her pocket.

"Good to go", she said. "Cappuccinos here we come".

We stood, we went out of her room, and I watched her lock the door. She paused.

"Nigel", she said, "What's happening is amazing".

" I know", I said.

SIX

There was a Costa coffee shop in the big Tesco store on the edge of town. Doctor Samuels and I spoke very little on the trip. Her car was an electric Nissan. We chatted a bit about how she was finding it after a petrol car. I always find these cars creepy to ride in, because they pull away from a standstill in total silence .... as though you are being pulled forwards by an invisible rope. By the time you reach 30mph, however, the tyre noise makes things sound more normal.

We walked into the store, and went straight upstairs.

"If you grab that corner table before it gets taken", she said, "I'll get the coffees".

It was just busy enough to ensure we could have a private conversation.

I established myself at the corner table. I sat there .... thinking .... until she appeared with the cappuccinos, and the lemon zesty tarts. You have to have lemon zesty tarts.

We sipped our coffees. Now Costa don't do anything very complicated .... but what they do .... they do very very well.

They charge you too much .... but get used to it. That's what they do.

"Will you tell me about the time you were scared", the Doctor said.

I buried my face in my hands. I felt the coffee doing what coffee does.

"Yes", I said, "I'll tell you".

She waited patiently sipping her coffee.

"Have you heard of the Great Dorset Steam Fair", I asked her.

"Yes, I've heard of it. I've even visited it", she said. "A huge fair in the countryside in Dorset. Lasts nearly a week"

"That's it". I said. "I used to run the best known of the antiques stalls there. "Nigel's Interesting Things" . I did it 9 times in a row. For us it was a ten day stay on site"

"I remember your stall", she said. "You had a big tipi as your accomodation".

"That's the one", I said.

"And this incident happened there, at the fair".

"On our first night on the site", I said.

"We would travel down with the trucks on the Friday evening . We weren't allowed onto our actual pitch until 8am on the Saturday morning , so our first night there was spent in what they called the "holding car park". I had quite a crew with me. Dave, driving the other truck, my girlfriend Jennifer, my assistant, young Isobel, and my partner on the stall, Laurence.

I would always cook a big chilli con carne in the morning, and finish it off in the caravan, and serve it for supper, over nachos, and we would have a few glasses of wine. Everybody would be in a party mood because all the stress of preparing, and getting there was over, and we could relax for the evening. Before the real work of setting up began the next morning.

I remember that particular evening being a lot of fun because two young antique dealers from London joined us for a couple of glasses of wine .... and of course they were chatting up Isobel because she was sort of gorgeous. But I have to emphasise that none of us were "pushing the boat out", because tomorrow, we all had a hard days work ahead of us, when we got on site.

So we got off to bed about 11.15 or so .... not late. Jennifer and I were in a little caravan we were using for that event .... not our normal big caravan. Dave was in the sleeper cab in one truck, Isobel in the other, and Laurence slept in his car.

The caravan had various items of stock in it, but we had a single bed each, on opposite sides of the van.

So everything was just fine, until about 1am .... I'm guessing the time. I woke up .... went to roll onto my side .... when suddenly the most unbelievable pain started in the upper part of my left leg".

"Your left thigh you mean", said Dr Samuels.

"Yes", I said. "It was cramp, muscle cramp, and it was very very bad. I'd experienced that cramp you get in your calves, when you're swimming, lots of times, but this was totally different .... a different level of pain completely".

"What did you do", she said.

"I went to get out of bed", I told her, "And then the same pain started in my right leg .... just the same. Then I knew something weird was happening. I wanted to get outside. See if I could move my legs around .... stretch them out .... try and relieve the pain .... which was getting stronger every second. I couldn't sit up .... the pain was too great. So I rolled out of the bed, and fell onto the floor. I dragged myself to the door, reached up, opened the latch, and crawled out onto the stubble field".

"What about Jennifer .... what was she doing", said Doctor Samuels.

"Absolutely fast asleep". I said

"So I'm laying on the stubble, in my T shirt and pants, and I dragged myself a few yards, and I was trying to move my legs.

And then the problem with my breathing started .... and that's the moment when I got really scared. I could only take shallow little breaths. So I had to try to breath more quickly, to get enough air, and I looked over to the security guard's hut, about a hundred yards away, and wondered if I could drag myself that far, and get them to radio for an ambulance or a doctor. I was in trouble .... lots of trouble .... and I needed help.

I'd just started to do it .... when the voice said .... quite clear, and very calm:

"Nigel .... if you want this to stop .... go and ask to hold your wife's hand".

Even at that moment .... trying to cope with the pain .... and scared about the breathing .... I noticed the oddness of the phraseology. Not "Go and hold Jennifer's hand", but "ASK to hold YOUR WIFE'S hand".

I never even thought to question it .... because I would have tried anything to free myself from that pain. I just dragged myself to the van .... managed to get back inside .... shook Jennifer awake .... and asked to hold her hand. I'm not sure she really woke up .... but she stretched out her hand .... and I held onto it".

Doctor Samuels leaned towards me.

"What happened", she asked.

"The pain stopped instantly". I said. "It just left me instantly .... and my breathing returned to normal at the same moment".

She stared at me, and shook her head.

"I went back to bed", I said, "and I was perfectly fine for the rest of the night .... in fact for the rest of the event".

She sat back, picking up her lemon zesty tart for the first time. I seemed to have eaten mine. I couldn't remember.

"Did you think about the incident the next day", she asked me.

"I asked Jennifer if she remembered anything", I said.

"And did she", asked the doctor.

"She remembered me asking to hold her hand .... and she asked me what it was all about".

"Did you tell her".

"To be honest", I said, "not really .... because we were flat out all next day. Setting up day is non stop work.

But in the quieter moments .... over the next week .... I began to really think about it .... to analyse it .... and to consider what I can't describe to you .... the strangeness of the incident".

"Did you reach a conclusion", she asked.

I looked at her. I finished my coffee. I smiled at her.

"Come on", I said. "You're a doctor .... does what I experienced remind you of anything".

She remained motionless, staring at me.

"It was a message .... a reminder .... wasn't it", she said.

I nodded:

"This is what I can do ....".

"With a capital I", said the Doctor.

"But "I" is always a capital letter", I said.

We lapsed into silence. The cups seemed to be empty.

"Shall I get us two more coffees", she asked

I nodded. She went. I felt the tears begin.

She returned. Two fresh cappuccinos.

"Share another zesty with me", she said.

I nodded.

"Have you made the connection since", she said.

"Yes I have", I said. "A year later .... and curiously .... it was at the same event".

"Can you tell me", she asked.

"Not now", I said.

She nodded .... accepting.

We munched our respective halves of a lemon zesty tart.

"The Magdalena tried to connect with you yesterday evening", she said, "but you only opened the door a fraction to her .... why".

"I'm in love with her", I said.

"I know", she said. "Tough break".

"Yeah", I said, "But ain't love grand".

"Spike .... Buffy the Vampire Slayer", she said.

I laughed.

"Spot on", I said.

"Do you think the Magdalena knows", she asked.

"Oh she knows", I said.

The Doctor gave me a questioning glance.

"The Magdalena said a final word to me, as she left the room, after dinner last night", I said.

"But you don't speak Aramaic", she said.

"Julie pretended she didn't hear the word". I said

"Ah", said the doctor.

"If we sit here any longer", I said, "We might as well order lunch".

She laughed.

"No", she said. "We'll have lunch with the Magdalena".

"Are you good to go".

"Yeah", I said. "Ain't love grand".

SEVEN

All Premier Travel Inns have a pub next door.

"We'll have lunch in the pub", said Doctor Samuels.

She put the Nissan silently into a parking space near the entrance.

"If you go and find us a table in a quiet corner", she said, "I'll fetch the Magdalena. Can you order two orange juices please .... and whatever you want".

She fished in her purse, and handed me a Premier Inn Privilege card.

"Open a tab with this card", she said. "The code is 0033".

I laughed.

"I know", she said. "But you have to pick a number you can remember".

As I went in, I realised the pub was a genuine old building. Probably a farm house, at least two hundred years old. There were plenty of nooks and crannies, and I found a table in a quiet corner quite easily. I layed my jacket on it, and went to the bar for the drinks. I asked to open a tab, and handed over the card. The bar maid swiped it.

She smiled at me.

"Any drinks to begin", she asked.

I ordered the orange juices, with ice, and added a Coke for myself".

"Drinks on the tab", she asked.

"Please", I said.

"Will you be eating", she asked.

"I believe we are", I said.

"Don't forget to bring your table number when you come to the bar to order", she said.

She gave me a tray. I took the drinks back to the table. Doctor Samuels, and The Magdalena, walked in a few moments later.

"Where's Julie", I said, standing to greet them.

"Having lunch with Peter and John", she said. "I wanted to give you and The Magdalena a chance to talk to each other".

"Despite the fact that I don't speak any Aramaic", I said.

"That's right Nigel", she said.

We sat. The Magdalena joined me against the wall, on the built in sofa. We sipped our drinks, and studied the lunch menu. The Magdalena pointed to a picture of an omelette with chips, and for the sake of simplicity, the Doctor and I decided to have the same.

I went to the bar.

"Hello again", said the barmaid. "What would you like .... you're on table 29 by the way. I spotted you when I was collecting glasses".

I ordered, and asked her to put it on the tab.

"All done", she said, "Have fun".

"Shouldn't you tell me to enjoy my lunch". I said

"I know you're going to enjoy your lunch", she said. She shot me a smile.

She was quite sassy. I liked her.

I returned to our table.

The Magdalena stood, She offered me her hands. I took them. I felt the Doctor watching us.

The Magdalena sank back to her seat, taking me with her. I opened the door .... and closed my eyes.

I got her calmness. Her extraordinary calmness .... and her acceptance. And I got joy. And I got Love. I sensed her immense love for Jesus. I showed her mine, and we stayed there .... until the word Love, and the name Jesus, came to mean the same thing for us.

And finally I got another thing. We were three. I looked at her ....
astonished. I went to let go of her hands, but she held me tightly. I felt her
urging me to go there .... into the mind of her unborn child .... into the
purest love that there could ever be.

It came through me, and over me, and round me, and time ceased to have
meaning. Three minds joined .... and The Magdalena urged me to join to
Him .... across space and time. But I wouldn't do it. I wouldn't open that
door. Not here.

She sighed and gently released my hands.

I needed a few minutes on my own. I knew the answer to one of the most
important questions concerning Jesus.

I mumbled an excuse. A few moments later I was staring at myself in the
mirror. I was younger. That briefest of touches had given me Life.

"I am the Way .... and I am the Truth .... and I am the Life".

I pulled myself together. Somehow ....

There were three ladies, and an omelette waiting for me. I returned to the
table. The Magdalena stood again, She smiled, took my hand, and placed
me on my seat. She sat.

Doctor Samuels stared at me .... and stared at me. She started to form a
question.

I shook my head at her. She lapsed into silence.

I wondered if she knew.

The omelettes arrived. The waiter placed our meals .... but The Magdalena
took control. She took the plates and put all three omelettes onto one plate,
and all the chips onto a second. She cut the food into small pieces with
her knife, then took all the cutlery from us, and wrapped in a knapkin. She
placed the two plates in the centre of the table, and offered each of us her
hands. She blessed the food, and signalled for us to begin. She led the way,

gently using her fingers. She was so elegant in her ways, that the Doctor and I felt embarrassed in our clumsy attempts to follow her example.

She laughed at us .... as She showed us how. She laughed at us .... and She laughed with her joy. And her joy laughed with her.

EIGHT

Doctor Samuels was fairly quiet as we walked back to the Hotel.

The Magdalena took my arm. I was surprised, but I thought that perhaps it might be natural in her culture.

But it was nice .... having her on my arm.

The Doctor asked about my business. I explained that my brother would take the reins in my absence.

"What's your brother like". she asked "Does he share your ability .... your gift".

"No", I said. "He doesn't".

"Does he know about you", she asked.

"No", I said. "He doesn't".

We lapsed into silence, until she keyed in the entrance code for the appartment.

"I'm intending to join you all for dinner this evening", she said. "I'll tell John".

The Magdalena spoke a few words, smiled, and headed for her room.

Back in the appartment, we found John at his lap top, and Peter sitting on the sofa reading a Bible. I guessed, from his page position, that he was brushing up his knowledge of the four Gospels.

They stood and greeted us. Doctor Samuels asked John about dinner. John disappeared off to the kitchen to organise with Simon.

"Which Gospel are you reading", I asked Peter.

"Mark", he said.

"That's the best Gospel", I said. "It really comes over that Mark was there".

"So you think Mark's Gospel is eye witness", said Peter.

"Definitely", I said. "Try reading 15:24 to 25".

There was silence .... while he read it .... and then read it again.

"I see what you mean", he said.

"What do you think of the other Gospels", said Doctor Samuels.

She came and sat down opposite Peter.

"Alright", I said, "John's is good .... it comes over as eye witness .... but it also comes over as an old man dictating his memoirs to a scribe, many years after the events. Sort of "My life with Jesus", but sitting back with his eyes closed, glass of wine in one hand, and a young scribe hanging on to his every word".

"Did they have wine glasses then", said Doctor Samuels, trying, and succeeding, in being annoying".

I ignored her.

"Luke", I said, "is the careful gospel writer .... very careful. And If you read carefully .... you'll notice that Luke doesn't have anybody eating or drinking anything at The Last Supper. Not that he was there of course".

"John was there though, wasn't he", said Doctor Samuels.

"He was". I said.

"So why didn't John talk about the bread and the wine being the flesh and the blood. He doesn't mention it at all. I always thought that was odd".

"He must have popped out for a minute", I said. "He missed that bit. Five minutes later, John comes back in, and says "Have I missed anything lads. Nah .... nothing important John", they say, "Just the instigation of the Holy Sacrament .... nothing important at all .... we'll fill you in later". It's so easy to forget these people were human like us .... all too easy to forget".

John came back in, and sat next to Peter.

"All Ok for dinner", he said "Eight o'clock alright".

"Good for me", said the doctor.

"Nigel", said Peter. "You haven't told us what you think of Mathew's Gospel yet....

Nigel has been giving us his take on the differences between the four Gospels", he explained to John.

"Ok .... Mathew ....", I said. "My least favourite of the four. Feels very distant from the events, second hand, even third hand narrative .... and far too much Old Testament spin".

"Old Testament spin", said the doctor, raising her eyebrows.

"Referring back to the Old Testament to prove Jesus is the prophesied Messiah", I said. "Mathew's Gospel does it so often, that it becomes tedious .... alright, alright, you begin to think .... we've got the message".

"Do you think Mathew the Disciple wrote it", asked John.

"No, definitely not", I said.

"Any idea who might have written it", said Peter, leaning forwards.

"I've always suspected Paul", I said. "He liked to write .... but nobody ever thinks, "Isn't it odd .... there's no Gospel of Paul". I don't think Paul could have resisted the temptation to write a full Gospel. I think he wrote Mathew .... but he didn't have the cheek to put his name on it. It's also interesting that Luke and Mathew are the most similar of the Synoptic Gospels. Mathew, Mark, and Luke .... that is".

"Because Paul and Luke were associates you mean" said Dr Samuel.

"Yes", I said "That very reason".

"I get the feeling you don't like Paul", said Peter.

"You'd be right", I said.

"Why not", said Doctor Samuels.

"Because we hear far too much of him, without any good reason", I said.

She raised her eyebrows. She was getting good at this. I was giving her plenty of practise.

"Right", I said "Doctor Samuels ....".

"You can call me Verena", she said "We're all in this for the long haul".

"Sorry .... Doctor Samuels", I said. "I grew up in a country village, and I was taught to give professional people their proper title. So the Doctor was Doctor Smith, and the Vet was Mr Smith, and the Nurse was Nurse Smith. That's the way it has to be".

"Were they really all called Smith", said the Doctor.

I gave her what I hoped was an appropriate glance.

"You were saying ....", she said.

"Yes, I was. Suppose you said to me. "Nigel, I'd like to learn about the war time Prime Minister, Winston Churchill. Have you got any books about him.

I'd say to you, yes, Doctor Samuels. I have two books about Winston Churchill. One by his wartime secretary who worked with him night and day throughout the war years .... and I've got a second book by somebody who didn't know Winston Churchill, never met Winston Churchill .... but claims to have had a vision of him.

Which book would you like to borrow from me".

"The first", said Doctor Samuels.

"Exactly", I said. "You wouldn't do it to Winston Churchill, so why do you do it to Jesus".

There was a silence.

"What really winds me up", I said, "is when a Church has a cross on the wall .... and then the preacher teaches from Paul. If you are going to teach Pauline Christianity .... take the cross down. Christianity is about Jesus' teachings. Not Paul's teachings. You go with Paul and you take a clear step away from Jesus .... and that's not the way to go .... it's the wrong direction".

They all thought about it ....

I capitalised on their silence.

"Nowhere", I said. "Absolutely nowhere, in those four Gospels, does Jesus say : "Paul is the way, the truth, and the life". He says, "I am the Way, the Truth, and the Life".

There was a long silence.

"I'm going to go and have a chat with the Magdalena", said Dr. Samuels.

We watched her go. Simon came in.

"It's tea time", he said, putting a tray with all the gear, on the coffee table. "And I've made some muffins, blueberry muffins .... I'll fetch them".

He returned with a dozen large muffins on a plate.

"Simon", said John, "We'll all get fat on your cooking".

"I can give you the number of a good personal trainer", said Simon. "I'll be in the kitchen if you need me".

We drank tea. We ate muffins. We waited for the ladies.

The muffins were the real thing. I went for a second.

"Where are you on The Gospel of Thomas", asked Peter.

"Best of the lot", I said. "Thomas worked with Jesus, and wrote down things He said. It doesn't get any better than that".

"Then you think the Thomas Gospel is genuine", asked John.

"I'm quite happy it's the real thing". I said "One hundred and fourteen sayings of Jesus".

"But why are you so convinced by it", said John.

I sighed. I considered a third muffin. I decided it would be downright sinful .... even if my digestive system was willing to attempt the task.

"Let's talk about The Thomas Gospel when the Magdalena is with us", I said, "Because She may actually have seen Thomas writing it. Now wouldn't that be something".

* * *

Doctor Samuels, Julie, and the Magdalena came into the room.

My heart only missed two beats this time. I would have to talk to the doctor about this.

The Magdalena was looking very modern .... in a cream blouse, black three quarter length skirt, lace patterned stockings, and court shoes. She was totally stunning, with those dark curls tumbling over her olive cheeks.

She spotted the muffins and pounced on them.

"Nothing wrong with Her appetite", said Doctor Samuels.

"Julie has been helping her work out some mediterranean recipes with Simon, but some of the ingredients are difficult for Julie to translate. She and Simon are going to go to a speciality grocery store to see if The Magdalena can identify things by sight".

I must have looked a little alarmed.

"Peter and Julie will go with them". said the Doctor.

The Magdalena came to me, with two muffins on a plate. She offered me one. I took it. She smiled. I smiled back.

Julie poured herself tea, and took a muffin.

"Julie", said Peter. "Could you ask the Magdalena if she knows the Disciple of Jesus called Thomas the twin, and if She does know him....has She ever seen Thomas writing down things Jesus says".

Julie spoke to the Magdalena. The Magdalena ate muffins and listened. She nodded, and spoke rapidly to Julie. Julie nodded once or twice, asked a final question, then turned to us.

We waited expectantly ....

Julie paused .... letting the tension mount.

"It's yes to both questions", she announced.

Peter laughed.

"Tell her that She has just made Nigel very happy", he said.

"Well .... myself .... and a lot of modern American Bible scholars", I said. "Particularly Elaine Pagels. Elaine Pagels was one of the first to believe the Gospel was genuine".

"So now we know", said John. "Quite a moment".

"I think there will be even better", I said.

I started on my third muffin .... the one The Magdalena had given me.

To this day, I probably remain the only person in the whole world, who has shared American muffins, with Mary Magdalene.

NINE

I had intended to borrow the car, and go home that afternoon. I needed more clothes. But somehow I just didn't want to . Simon was going to Tescos for shopping, so I went with him, and for no huge amount of money, I bought myself a reasonable variety of shirts and trousers, socks, underwear, and a new jacket. I was on a hundred a day expenses after all.

I liked Simon. I asked him how he'd got the job.

"I was working at a mediterranean food restaurant in the West End", he told me. "John came in one night. He had a meal. He came back two nights later with Peter, and they both had a meal. They asked if they could meet the Chef .... being myself. They offered me double whatever my salary was, to work for them. Easy decision. I stayed where I was for a week, briefed my replacement, and started cooking for John and Peter. Julie and the Magdalena came a few days later, and then Doctor Samuels .... although she doesn't always eat with us".

"Simon, are you religious", I asked.

"Not sure I'm religious", he said, "But I know there is a God".

"How do you know there is a God", I asked.

He smiled at me.

"I looked at Julie", he said. "Only God can do that with molecules".

"You're right Simon". I said. "Only God can do that".

* * *

Back at the hotel, I helped Simon carry his shopping to the kitchen. I left him putting things in cupboards, and went back to the car for my own purchases. Having left the car keys on the hall table, I went back to my bedroom, and started taking the labels off my new clothes.

Simon had mentioned a laundry room, off the entrance hall, and I put my original clothes in to wash. I decided to lay down for a while. Relax before the evening. It would be nice to fall asleep for a while, but the two coffees in the morning were probably going to make that next to impossible.

I lay on the bed. Then I decided to do something I didn't often feel the need to do nowadays: I would pray.

Mention praying to most people, and they think of that excruciatingly boring business you have to do in Church. And its just too embarrassing. And then .... horror of horrors .... when some people start doing it on their knees .... well it just makes you cringe to think about it.

Or they think of children being taught to say their prayers at bedtime, kneeling, in best victorian fashion, by their beds. With clean shiny faces .... and palms pressed together

I hadn't prayed like that for a long time. Why didn't I pray like that any more ....

Because I lived with Him as part of my everyday life .... so the conversation was constant .... and ongoing. From the moment .... several years before .... in the bitter cold of a February evening .... when I had finally said to Him:

"Ok .... I give up. I surrender. If You want me .... I'm Yours".

I remember a friend, an African Pastor, saying in one of his Sermons on a Wednesday evening:

"If you stop listening to God .... He'll stop talking to you. Would you continue to talk to somebody who doesn't listen to you. No .... why would you. Listen to God. He'll keep talking to you .... while you keep listening to Him".

It was Pastor John Paul Oddoye, and later that year, I let him baptise me .... in the sea at Sandbanks .... on the Dorset coast.

I wouldn't let just anybody Baptise me. It had to be a true man of God.

So now I talked to God as an ongoing thing .... and God talked to me .... and I listened. It worked well for both of us. And my life had changed. Never a dull moment.

But now, in that Premier Travel Inn upper room, I decided to do it the old fashioned way. I was lacking a Victorian night shirt, but I knelt at the side of the bed, pressed my hands together, and prayed.

I talked to God. We had stuff to talk about. He always has the time.

*   *   *

I must have fallen asleep. I didn't really remember.

Peter put his head round the door at 7 o'clock.

I showered .... experimented with my new wardrobe .... and ended up in black trousers, and a pale blue shirt. Again, I tucked my cross safely out of sight.

I joined John and Peter in the living room, just as Doctor Samuels arrived. She went to find The Magdalena and Julie, and a few moments later we were all assembled on the sofas. John poured from a jug of tonic water, I could hear the ice tinkling. He handed us each a glass.

We sat and waited for Simon to call us for Dinner.

TEN

Simon called us through to dinner on the dot of eight pm. We kicked off with a spicy vegetable soup. There was no wine on the table, but Simon had provided a large jug of iced water, and several different fruit juices.

I mentioned the lack of wine, and was astounded to discover that, like myself, none of my companions drank alcohol .... apart from The Magdalena.

But Doctor Samuels would not allow her to drink.

"Far to young", she said to me, and gave me a quick glance that stifled any comment I had been about to make.

"I agree", I told her. I noticed a flicker of a smile from John.

Simon cleared the soup bowls. The Magdalena spoke rapidly to Julie, who excused herself from the table, and went through to the kitchen.

The Magdalena stood, motioning us to remain seated, as was her habit, and came around the table, collecting our cutlery.

John and Peter watched this with puzzled expressions.

Placing the cutlery on the side table, The Magdalena came to me.

"Nigel", she said, "Please stand".

It was my turn to be puzzled. I was thrilled to hear her use my name, and I supposed that she had asked Julie to teach her some English words.

She turned me round to the light, reached up, and pushed up my shirt collar. She loosened the two top buttons and drew out the chain, with it's cross, from under my shirt. She put the chain around my neck .... but, this time, over my shirt .... fastened the buttons again .... and turned my collar down neatly. My cross now hung in plain view.

She smoothed my shirt.

"Nigel", she said "Be brave .... for me".

Her accent made the words hang in the air.

"Thank you", I said.

We sat again, and Simon, and Julie, came through from the kitchen. They carried three plates each. Simon asked us to clear a space in the middle of the dining table. He and Julie layed the plates in a line along the centre. He had cooked a paella, and cut it into bite sized pieces. The other three plates held salad, very colourful, and chopped small.

"Are we using our fingers then", said John.

"I'm afraid we are", said Doctor Samuels. "Nigel and I had the opportunity to practise at lunch. You'll get the hang of it in no time".

"Even if you don't eat as elegantly as the Magdalena does", I added.

The Magdalena motioned us to rise, and said a blessing.

It was much shorter than yesterday. We looked to Julie.

"Where two share a plate, then two will be fed, instead of one .... and she thanks God for this blessing of food".

We began to eat, Doctor Samuels and I rather more at ease than John, Peter, and Julie.

"I always thought that the concept of two sharing a plate was Islamic in origin", said Doctor Samuels.

"Islam is six hundred years in the future for our guest", said Peter.

"Ah", said the Doctor. "Of course it is .... sorry".

"Nigel", said Peter. "We'll do as yesterday, and leave the planning until The Magdalena and Julie have left us. There are inevitably going to be parts of our talk tonight that are in the future for The Magdalena, and although Julie could simply choose not to translate those parts .... I would feel more comfortable if we were on our own .... although Doctor Samuels is going to stay with us tonight".

I had been wondering about this problem myself, so I was happy to go along with Peter's suggestion of keeping the planning for later.

I turned to Julie and asked her if The Magdalena would answer a question about Jesus. It was a question that might have some bearing on our plans .... but let's face it .... it was also a question that every Bible historian in the World would give his eye teeth to have the answer to.

Julie asked The Magdalena, who blushed, but nodded her assent, and then, prompted by Julie, she said haltingly:

"Yes Nigel".

I took the plunge.

"Does The Magdalena know where Jesus lived between the ages of fourteen and twenty nine", I asked.

Julie considered for a moment.

"The Magdalena doesn't think of age, in terms of years, in the simple way we do", she said. "I'm going to have to phrase this carefully, so that she understands what you want to know".

She turned to The Magdalena. They began a conversation that lasted several minutes, and became quite animated.

We all waited for the outcome, continuing with the meal, and feeling considerable relief when Simon appeared with more knapkins. Eating with our fingers was going to take some getting used to.

"Get with the program", said Simon. "I'm not going to lay cutlery at all from now on".

"Are you serious", said Peter.

"Afraid so", said Simon. "Saves me having to wash it up".

John and Peter sighed.

Doctor Samuels and I smiled in a superior sort of way. I know we shoudn't have .... but we did.

Eventually Julie turned back to us.

"I'm not at all sure that I have understood this", she said.

"I asked The Magdalena when She first met Jesus. Were they children when they first met. The problem is that She simply doesn't see the distinction between childhood, and adulthood, in the same way that we do. But She is certain that She first met Jesus just before the ceremony where He became a Man .... in other words, He entered adulthood. That would be at thirteen years of age in our thinking. She became very friendly with Jesus, and saw Him often over the next year or so. Then His Uncle Joseph ....".

"Joseph of Arimathea", I asked.

"Yes", said Julie. "Joseph of Arimathea. His Uncle took him on a trip that lasted nearly two years".

Julie had our full attention now.

"The Magdalena doesn't know how to name the country they travelled to, but when Jesus described it to her, He said that it was a very wet country, with fields of green grass, and tall green leafed trees, and streams and rivers and flooded land. And in the Winter it became so cold that the rain fell as large white flakes, and the water in pools became hard as iron. The people there did not worship the One True God, but worshipped the Sun, and the Wind, and things of nature".

"Could it have been England", said John, "Glastonbury in Somerset..............".

"The Festival, you mean", said Julie brightly.

"Julie !!!!!", we all said.

"Sorry", she said, "I coudn't resist that. He would have been right at home at Glastonbury Festival".

"You said they were away for two years", I prompted her.

"Yes", said Julie, "Then Jesus was at home for another year or so before his Uncle took Him away on another trip".

We all leant towards her.

"Where to this time", asked Peter.

"Again, The Magdalena can't give us a recognisable name for the country, but she is emphatic on one point. Jesus didn't return this time .... not until He was a fully grown man. And He had changed very much while He was away. What He said and What He thought, and how He acted. In fact He had changed into the Jesus She fell in love with .... and the Jesus we know".

"So He didn't grow into adulthood in The Holy Land", said John. "But where was He".

"John", I said. "Suppose I disappeared from my home village when I was fourteen, stayed away fifteen years, then came back and opened the most utterly amazing pizza and pasta restaurant. Where might I have been".

"Italy", said John.

"It's not difficult to work out where He was", I said.

*　*　*

Simon served a baked alaska for the dessert dish. I hadn't seen one of these since the late nineteen seventies, so it was quite a novelty .... and it thrilled the Magdalena when she cut through the hot sponge, to discover the ice cream centre. Despite his threat about the cutlery, Simon had relented and allowed us to use spoons for the dessert. He served us each a tiny cup of hot chocolate to conclude the meal, and as before, Julie and The Magdalena stood to leave us. But this time The Magdalena hesitated at the table.

"Nigel please come", she said.

I looked at Julie and raised my eyebrows.

"The Magdalena would like you to escort her to her room", said Julie. She wants to pray with you".

"Are you joining us", I asked.

"No", she said. "You'll be just fine on your own".

The Magdalena led me to her room, held the door open for me, and motioned that I should enter.

Her room was sweet with her perfume. Everything was very neat .... just the wardrobe door ajar. She had an impressive collection of clothes. She and Julie must have made some serious shopping trips.

She closed the door behind us, then came and stood in front of me. Her delicate olive skinned fingers lifted the cross from my shirt front. She stood there, looking at the symbol, then I noticed the tears on her cheeks. She cried softly .... and I took her gently in my arms and held her.

I'd never had children. I would have liked a daughter. But for those few moments another man's daughter held me in her arms. She started to pray. I joined Her.

There's a saying.

"It's strange what a man will do, for a bite of bread, and another man's daughter".

ELEVEN

I returned to the dining room, and told Julie that The Magdalena was waiting for her. Julie said goodnight to us.

"Did you pray together", she asked me.

"We did", I said.

"Will you pray with me tomorrow", she asked.

"I'd like that very much", I said.

She left us then. But her White Linen perfume stayed with us.

* * *

I joined John, Peter, and Doctor Samuels, at the table. Peter was pouring coffee. He handed me a cup. We sat and looked to each other.

"Nigel", asked John. "Do you think we should rescue Jesus".

His question surprised me. I thought we were agreed on it.

"Yes I do", I said. "He wasn't meant to die on the cross".

"And do you believe we can do it", said John.

"Well yes", I said, "But there are two options. With the technology you have, you could lift Him from first Century Jerusalem well before His arrest. But that would alter history. Probably alter the Christian faith out of all recognition. I'm assuming we do not want to do that, because the consequences are incalculable".

"They are", said John, "and you're right, we can't do that".

"In that case, then", I said,"I can see just one tiny window of opportunity for us to get Him out of the mess He's in .... and, with luck, we should leave history intact".

"You're talking about the spear thrust", said John.

"I am", I said.

"We'd reached the same conclusion", said Peter, "but perhaps via a different route to yourself".

"If that spear thrust hadn't happened", I said, "Jesus would have "died" after drinking the "vinegar". Pontious Pilate would have released the body to Joseph and Nicodemus. They would have taken Jesus down, after just six hours on the cross, and taken Him to the tomb.

They could treat His wounds, and wait for Him to revive, in the privacy of that tomb".

"But the spear thrust still has to happen", said Doctor Samuels.

"I know it does", I said, "because that spear thrust is clearly described in the Gospel accounts of the crucifixion, and it crops up again when Thomas wishes to see Jesus' wounds in the upper room".

"So accepting that the spear thrust must happen", said John,"Do we have a solution".

"There is a way", I said. "We have to have control of that spear .... and that means we have to have control of that Roman soldier".

"Ah", said John, "I think I can see what you have in mind".

"John", I said, "I think you might have Military connections. Can you get us a young special forces officer".

"I know a man who can", said John. "But what nationality would he be".

"That's a very good question", I said. "We need somebody to advise us .... and just like you .... I know a man who can".

Peter fetched a lap top to the table, and, on my instructions, went to Google, and tapped in "Ermine Street Guard".

"And who are "The Ermine Street Guard", said John.

"They're into military re-enactment", I said. "To be specific .... ancient Roman military re-enactment .... but they are really serious about it. Their clothing, their armour, their weapons .... all have to be absolutely authentic. They spend a lot of time on research, to make sure it's all period correct".

The website came up. We went to the Gallery pages and I could tell that John and Peter were impressed by what they saw. We went to the "Contact us" page next. I was disappointed not to find a phone number, but there were several email addresses. The list was headed by their officer in overall command .... and it was the name I wanted to see .... Chris Haines.

I took over from John and wrote an email to Chris, reminding him of old times, and asking him to contact me urgently on my mobile number. I checked what I had written .... pressed send .... and sat back.

"So you know their commanding officer", said John.

"I do", I said, "And for a long time. Chris is a pig farmer in Herefordshire. A really lovely down to earth chap, and he started The Guard about thirty five years ago. They are now considered to be the leading experts on Roman military history".

My phone rang. It couldn't be ....

It was Chris Haines himself. Same Hereford accent. Same Chris.

We chatted about old times, about a mutal friend .... a certain armourer .... and eventually Chris asked how he could help me.

I explained the information we needed. Chris thought for a moment.

"You need to talk to Eric Wilson about this. He's our historian. I'm not supposed to give you his number, but I'll phone him now, and if he's in, and he probably will be, I'll get him to ring you back. I'll phone back myself later to see if you got what you wanted".

"Before you go Chris", I said, "If we make progress with this project, would you be willing to train and advise a first century Roman soldier for us. He'll be a real soldier from one of the special forces".

"If he's a real soldier, then we're more than half way there before we start", said Chris. "Soldiering hasn't changed that much in two thousand years".

"And Chris", I said, "There's a fairly serious budget for this project, so we can negotiate a fee for your organisation".

"I like what I hear Nigel", he said, "I'll get Eric to phone you".

Just a few minutes later my phone rang again. I looked at the others. We were on a roll.

It was Eric Wilson.

We chatted. He explained his roll in The Guard. Then I asked him our question.

"Ok", he said. "First century Holy Land. Roman occupying forces. What sort of soldiers would have executed Jesus of Nazareth. Obviously a Centurion in command, but an execution detail was always professional soldiers, not conscripts .... to much chance of local sentiments messing things up. Jesus would have been seen as a political prisoner, so I would expect all Roman soldiers .... the real thing. Hard as nails. No pandering to local feelings. Physical type .... Italian, or Spanish possibly .... stocky build, dark hair, clean shaven. Might have picked up some of the local lingo, depending on how long he'd been posted there, but safer to assume he'd speak basic soldiers Latin".

I made notes on a pad that Peter had passed to me. We had what we wanted. I thanked Eric, told him I was going to speak to Chris again, and rang off.

Chris hadn't withheld his number, so I rang him back and said that Eric had given us the information we needed.

"Chris", I said, "If we can find our soldier .... can we deliver him to you for training, his uniform, and his equipment".

"I can't wait to see an SAS officer in a skirt", said Chris.

"And Chris", I said. "He'll need training in the use of the pilum".

"The pilum ....", said Chris. "Nigel .... just what have you got yourself into".

"Chris .... if I'm allowed to tell you .... I will", I said.

I said goodbye .... and ended the call.

"Life's all about who you know", I said.

"I'll start making some calls", John said. "I'd like our soldier here by tomorrow evening".

Peter poured us all a second coffee, and went to the kitchen for the posh biscuits. We had a workable plan.

84

TWELVE

I didn't hurry to get up the next morning. Simon brought croissants with bacon, and a pot of tea. He stayed and chatted while I ate.

"John went off early this morning .... about seven", he told me.

"Ah yes", I said. "Gone to see a man about a soldier. We might have an extra guest for dinner this evening".

"I usually have tonight off", said Simon. "It'll have to be take-away for you all tonight".

"I'll go and get it", I said. "I know all the best ones".

"I'm only joking", said Simon, "I don't mind staying .... I didn't have anything planned yet".

"What would you have done", I asked him.

"Usually go out for a drink with a friend. He's a Chef. We swap recipes".

* * *

I went through to the living room with him, and found Julie finishing her breakfast. I sat down with her. She poured me a tea.

"Will you really pray with me", she said.

"Yeah, no problem at all", I said.

"When can we do it", she said.

"Right here, right now, if you like", I said.

"I don't know how to pray", she said. "I just feel self conscious and stupid when I try".

I smiled.

"Do you feel self conscious and stupid talking to me", I said.

"Of course not", she said.

"Why not", I asked.

"Because you're here, and I can see you", she said.

"Would you talk to me on the phone", I asked.

"Yes" she said.

"But you wouldn't be able to see me then", I said.

"Don't be silly", she said. "I know you exist".

"Ah", I said. "Now we have the real problem .... you don't know that God exists .... so you aren't sure if anybody is actually listening when you are praying".

She was silent.

"Well even if I was absolutely sure He existed", she said. "Why would He be listening to me, when there are so many other people praying to Him".

"Depends where He is", I said.

"Well He's in Heaven isn't He", she said.

"But suppose He left a little part of Himself inside you", I said. "Now do you think He'll hear you".

She thought about that.

"You really do believe in God Don't you", she said.

"No Julie", I said. "I don't believe in God".

She turned to me in astonishment.

"But........".

"People believe lots of things", I said, "But you can believe wrong things very easily .... that's how betting shops make their money. People believe a horse is going to win a race. They believe it strongly enough to risk money on it …. and they lose their money. Just because you believe a thing …. it doesn't make it true".

"Oh" she said. "I never thought of it like that".

"Julie …. I know there is a God", I said. "And I'm happy to say to you: "Julie …. there really is a God, and He really will listen to you if you pray to Him".

She sat staring at me.

"You really mean that don't you".

"I do".

She thought.

"Ok then" she said. "Show me how to do it …. show me how you pray".

"Just talk to God, like you're talking to me".

"But don't I have to do it in a religious way, and pray for other people".

"If you were God, Julie,", I said. "Would you rather that You heard prayers being said for John, and Peter …. or would You rather John, and Peter, came to You in prayer for themselves".

"I'd rather they came to Me themselves", she said.

"Ok", I said "away you go then".

"How do I start", she said.

"Just say, "Good morning Awesome God", I said.

"Do I have to say it out loud", she said.

"I won't hear it if you don't", I said. "You asked me to pray with you …. remember".

"Will God hear me, if it's not out loud", she asked.

"Julie", I said, "Just get on with it".

* * *

Half an hour later I was perfectly happy that Julie and God had swapped email addresses, and that their laptops were talking to each other. Julie seemed surprised that praying really was that easy.

"I'm going to spend a bit of time in my room with it", she said.

As she left the room she turned.

"Nigel, do you ever go to a Church to pray", she asked.

"Now that's an interesting question", I said. "Can I answer that later".

She nodded, and headed for her room. I headed for the bathroom.

I found Peter in the living room when I returned. He was eating his breakfast. He had just poured me a tea, when his phone rang. He picked it up, glancing at the screen.

"It's John", he said.

"John .... it's Peter", he said. He listened .... then held his phone out to me.

"John wants to talk to you", he said.

I took the phone .... one of the new large screen models.

"John", I said. "How's it going".

"Good morning Nigel", said John, "Not bad .... I'm sitting here with a commanding officer I happen to know. He has suggested we meet a Captain in his regiment .... a certain Marco Rossi. He's twenty five, has an Italian Father, and an English Mother, takes after his Father in looks. And he has a degree in history .... believe it or not.

I'm told he is very resourceful, which sounds good, and his commander here tells me he can charm the birds down from the trees .... and this is the really good bit .... he can charm the birds down from the trees in Latin. He speaks several languages".

"Let's book him John", I said.

"There's a problem", said John.

"And the problem is ....", I asked.

"He's Roman Catholic".

"Ah", I said. "Is he a practising Roman Catholic".

"Yes", said John.

"Oh bother", I said.

"That's a Winnie the Pooh expression isn't it", said John.

"Yes", I said.

"What do you want me to do", said John.

I thought.

"Do we know what period of history he studied".

John conferred. There was a pause.

"It's not on this record", said John, "but we think it's European mediaeval. His commander here remembers a conversation in the mess one evening".

I thought again .... then I remembered our trump card. The Magdalena.

"I think we should go for it", I said. "We've got The Magdalena".

"I was thinking the same thing myself", said John. "I'll sort the details out, and phone Peter later".

I handed the phone back to Peter, and sat back on the sofa. My tea was cold.

Peter wound up the call, and sat down.

"John has found us the perfect man", I said. "Ticks every box .... just one problem".

"I know", said Peter, "but if we wanted an Italian, then there was always a strong chance he'd be a Catholic".

I nodded.

"We've got The Magdalena", said Peter.

I laughed.

"Yes", I said, "We have The Magdalena".

This was going to be very interesting.

FOURTEEN

John phoned us at lunch time. He had met Mark Rossi. Mark had been willing to listen to a proposal for a special assignment, and his commanding officer had granted him leave. John intended to bring Mark to the apartment for dinner. They hoped to arrive at about 6.30pm, and it was agreed that Mark would stay overnight.

Peter went down to organise a room for him in the hotel. We had run out of rooms in the apartment.

We had a free afternoon.

John walked into the apartment at 6 o'clock. He had seen Mark into his room on the floor below, and left him to shower and change.

At a quarter to seven we all assembled in the lounge. The Magdalena however stayed in her room. She would wait to be called. Julie had explained the situation to her, and she understood why we preferred to do things this way.

At seven, there was a tap on the door. John had gone to fetch Mark, and we looked up with great interest as he showed the young man into the room.

For some reason. I had expected him to be in uniform, but he wasn't. I know just enough about clothes to recognise Italian fashion. Mark obviously knew a lot about clothes. He was smart casual. Italian Smart Casual, and that is very smart. His Italian blood was obvious, with dark wavy hair, olive skin, and despite his obvious fitness, he was a little stockier for his height, than you would expect to see in an English man of his age.

I loved his clothes. If he set out to create the appearance of a mercenary officer on an evening out, he had achieved it perfectly. A soft brown suede tight wasted jacket, over a cream open neck shirt. Very fitted dark trousers, and very sharp Italian designer shoes.

I glanced to our ladies. They were liking what they saw.

"Ladies and Gentlemen", said John. "May I present Captain Mark Rossi. SAS".

Mark smiled round at us all.

"I'm pleased to meet friends of John's" he said. "But please .... from now on .... call me Mark".

His accent was English public school, but there was just a hint of Latin exotic in the delivery.

"Mark", said John. "This is the team".

Mark glanced round at us. It might have appeared to be a casual glance .... but he didn't miss a thing. He was obviously well trained in appraising people quickly.

"Can I introduce you to my co-director, Peter White", said John, "He and I will be dealing with the technical side of the operation".

Mark shook his hand.

"And this is our special advisor to the project, Nigel White".

Mark gave me a questioning look.

"No", said John, "not related".

"And", he said, "I'll have to apologise for leaving the ladies to last .... but this is Doctor Verena Samuels, our medical advisor".

The Doctor stepped forward and shook Mark's hand. She seemed very happy with the way things were going.

" Ah .... the Medic", said Mark, "Doctor Samuels, I'm pleased to meet you .... but I shall do my very best to ensure that our relationship remains a social one".

The Doctor laughed.

"And finally", said John, "We have Miss Julie Parker-Smith, from the languages department of Cambridge University. Julie is our linguistics expert".

Mark had shaken hands with each of us in turn. He paused when he reached Julie.

"Languages", he said, taking her hand.

If I told you that she smiled at him .... yes, that would be true .... but if I told you that she melted .... well, that would give you a much better picture of her reaction.

He spoke to her in French. She replied in German. He smiled, changed to Spanish, and she retorted in Russian. He paused, and then spoke in Latin. She replied in Aramaic.

He laughed.

"Julie", he said. "You win .... I didn't recognise a single word of that".

"Aramaic", she said blushing with delight.

I began to wonder, as I'm sure the others were wondering, just how long Mark was going to hold on to Julie's hand. Reluctantly he released her, and I'm sure she was equally reluctant to be released.

John seized the moment to suggest that we all sat down. Julie moved quickly aside for Mark. I lost out on that round of musical chairs, and had to cross to the other sofa to join John and Peter.

"Well", said Mark, "What a very interesting combination of skills and talents. So what is the project objective".

We looked to John.

"Before you begin John", I said. "May I ask a question".

John motioned me to go ahead.

"Captain Rossi .... sorry .... Mark", I said. "I understand that you are a practising Roman Catholic .... is that correct".

Whatever Mark had expected me to say .... it wasn't that.

He laughed.

"Yes", he said, "Practising is correct .... but I'm not very good at it .... and I don't intend to be".

He looked round at our surprised faces.

"I can see you haven't got the full story", he said, "And that's just fine. It means my cover is working".

We stared at him, wondering what was coming.

"My Mother and Father are very devout Roman Catholics", he said. "And they are really lovely people, and I would always wish to love and respect them".

We nodded approval.

"Do you know I have a degree in History", he asked.

Again we nodded.

"Yes" he said. "It was a really interesting course .... but it did leave me with certain avenues of research I wanted to explore .... especially concerning the Church of Rome".

"And this research led you to change your views", I asked trying to hide the hopeful tone in my voice.

"It did", he said. "And although I do attend Mass with my parents when I'm at home .... I am, in fact, much more at ease with a more modern style of worship. When I'm stationed at our home base, I have a favourite Church that I'm very fond of".

"Is it a Pentecostal Church, by any chance", I asked.

It was his turn to look surprised.

"No need to be surprised", I said. "My favourite Church is a Pentecostal Church, and we have lots of Catholics who have found their way there".

He reached over and shook my hand, smiling with pleasure.

"Amen to that", he said.

We all sat back in our chairs. Our relief must have been obvious. This wasn't going to be a difficult as we'd feared.

He noticed that we had relaxed.

"Was it something I said", he asked.

We laughed.

"John", I said. "It's your turn".

John explained the proposed mission.

The next ten minutes were very much like the scene in my home, when John and Peter had first visited me.

I saw Mark's expression of complete incredulity .... I saw him decide that we were all completely crazy. Then I saw his mounting curiosity, as he looked round at us .... and finally I saw him conclude, that despite himself, he was interested enough, to hear more.

And then, we reached the point beloved of TV show directors.

The Reveal.

Julie went to fetch The Magdalena.

Mark jumped to his feet as She entered. As She crossed the room to meet him, we all stood.

John introduced her by her correct name: Mary of Magdala. Mary Magdalene.

The effect on Mark was interesting to watch. He stood transfixed looking at her face. I saw plainly the moment when he realised that everything he had heard from us was actually real.

He sank to his knees before her and bowed his head.

The Magdalena, as was her style, laid a hand on his head, and blessed his presence.

She cast us a puzzled glance.

"I really must explain this to her at some point", I heard Julie say, under her breath.

But we were overjoyed. Mark was with us now .... to the end.

*   *   *

The meal that evening was a lot of fun. I had thought that Mark might want to ask questions, but he seemed happy to take his cue from the rest of us, and we managed to keep the conversation well clear of the project.

He would also have understood the implications of The Magdalena being with us.

He lost no opportunity to flirt with Julie. He had an air of absolute confidence that if attractive, as it obviously was, to Miss Parker-Smith, it was also very reassuring for the rest of us.

FIFTEEN

Our Chef did us proud that evening. He presented us with the best spaghetti bolognese I've ever eaten .... and as it happens to be my favourite meal .... I've eaten quite a few.

I holidayed on the Greek Island of Lesvos once. I ate the same spaghetti bolognese, in the same restuarant, every evening of my ten day stay. I would walk in each evening, determined to try something different. I would study the menu. I would consider something different.

But .... suppose I didn't like it as much as the spaghetti bolognese ....

Mark insisted that we stand for the Magdalena to bless the food. With her permission, via Julie, he added a Grace in Italian, and we sat.

We used normal cutlery for our bolognese, even The Magdalena seeming to know when she was well and truly beaten. Julie showed her how to wind the spaghetti round her fork .... Simon had served it full length .... but in the end, she took The Magdalena's plate, and cut the pasta into short lengths. We were all very relieved.

Simon seemed pleased when Mark complimented him on the dish, assuming for the purpose, a quite outrageous Italian accent.

"Will you give me the recipe Simon", he asked.

Simon looked horrified.

"I suppose", he said, "that we might discuss terms later".

He returned to his kitchen.

"I have to say", said Mark, turning to John, "you know how to build a team".

"I've had help", said John.

"Should that have been a capital H there, John", I asked.

"Perhaps", said John.

Simon brought in a very simple dessert of real Italian ice cream. Very dense, white as snow, and creamy beyond expectation. He gave us dishes of assorted sprinkles to top it.

Now real, and I mean real, Italian ice cream, is quite an experience the first time you encounter it. I watched with interest to see how The Magdalena would react to her first spoon full. I was not disappointed. She spoke to Julie, her face alive with pleasure.

"The Magdalena loves the ice cream, Simon", said Julie.

"Any chance of a flake Simon", said Mark .... pushing his luck.

"They were fresh out", said Simon. "Coffee to finish ....".

As always, The Magdalena was forbidden coffee, and not long after finishing her dessert, she made it apparent that She would leave us. We all stood, and Mark took her hand and wished her the sweetest dreams .... in Spanish.

Julie translated, and followed her from the room. I wondered if tonight, Miss Parker Smith might find reason to join us again. A few minutes later she returned to the table.

"I've left The Magdalena to pray", she explained.

*   *   *

We sat back. Peter poured coffee for us all.

"Well", said Mark, "What exactly is it you want me to do".

John explained what we needed.

"So", said Mark, "You want me to remove one combatant from the scene, substitute myself, and administer that famous spear thrust .... but in a non lethal fashion".

"In a nutshell, yes", said John.

"As SAS operations go", said Mark. "Nice easy little job .... no problems".

We loved his confidence.

"What do I do after completing my task", said Mark.

"As soon as you can, lose your uniform, and get back to the rest of the team", said John.

"And they'll be at the Tomb, I'm guessing", said Mark.

"In theory, yes", said John.

"Might be an idea to retain my gear then", said Mark. "A Roman soldier on guard outside would be reassuring for the rest of you".

"But that could be risky for you", I said.

"Look", said Mark. "I'm a professional soldier, and the welfare and safety of the team are my responsibility, until I'm relieved of duty. Thats the way it always is …. Period".

We fell silent. We realised that this young man had been in real situations that the rest of us would only see in movies, or read about in novels.

John nodded.

"Mark", he said. "I'm happy to hand over control of the military aspects of the project to you".

There was a silence. We looked to Mark.

"Good to go", he said.

"Doctor Samuels", said Mark, "Where do you want that spear thrust to go, so that it's non lethal …. and have you got a spear for me to examine".

John explained about Chris Haines, and The Ermine Street Guard.

"I've actually seen them in action", said Mark, "at a Military tattoo. They are so realistic, it's scary".

"So by tomorrow night", he said, "I'll be wearing a short skirt, and waving a spear about".

"If your friends could only see you ....", said Doctor Samuels.

"Again Doc",said Mark. "Where do you want me to poke this spear .... because the success of the op. seems to depend on me getting that right".

The Doctor looked to Peter.

"Peter", she said, "Do we have a felt tipped marker pen here .... a fairly large one".

"I've got one", said John. He fetched his briefcase from the lounge, and handed the Doctor a large pen".

"Now Mark", she said, "Would you mind removing your shirt for me please".

John and Peter seemed suddenly very busy with their coffee. Poor Julie was doing her best. She was going to get a grandstand view.

I looked at the Doctor. There was a distinct twinkle in her eyes. She had done this deliberately for Julie.

You had to hand it to Mark .... his confidence was unassailable.

"With your permission ....", he said, smiling at poor Miss Parker Smith.

She nodded, blushing, perfectly aware that Mark had noticed her confusion.

Mark stood, stepped away from the table, and without the slightest hesitation, removed his shirt.

We'd realised he was fit. Now we could see he was indeed very very fit. I glanced at Julie, who had obviously decided it was best to just go with the flow.

It was Doctor Samuels turn to stand. She went around the table to Mark, paused in front of him, and used the marker pen to draw a three inch line on his side.

"We need a cut, rather than an actual thrust", she said. "We need enough blood to make it convincing".

"What about the water", I said.

"That", she said, "we are going to have to leave to the artistic licence of the Gospel writers. I've always been puzzled by the water. I don't think it's important enough for us to worry about".

Mark examined the black line on his side.

"It's going to be all about where you are standing, so you can get the best angle", said the Doctor, helpfully.

"With you there", said Mark. "I'll work it out with The Guard, when I've got a spear in my hand. How long will this line stay there .... before it wears off".

"About a year", said John. "That's an indelible marker".

"Fine", said Mark. "May I put my shirt back on please".

"You may", said Doctor Samuels, smiling .... contentedly.

"Would you like Julie to help you with the buttons ....".

"Do you know .... I believe I would", he said. He raised his eyebrows in Julie's direction.

She took a deep breath. There was no way out for her. If she was going to retain her dignity .... well .... there was no choice. She went to Mark, slowly fastened his buttons from bottom to top, tucked him in, and smoothed the result.

"There you go soldier", she said.

"Thank you Julie", he said.

"A pleasure Sir", she said. We noticed a distinct hint of Victorian housemaid.

Mark and Julie rejoined us at the table.

*   *   *

"Miss Parker Smith", said Mark, as we stood to retire a short time later.

"I am unfamiliar with the layout of this hotel, and I wondered if I might presume upon your kindness, to show me to my room".

Julie hadn't quite got used to this young man's confidence yet. But she wasn't going to feel foolish in front of him.

"I would be delighted, Captain Rossi", she said.

I pondered deeply on Mark's SAS training in reaching distant locations .... under combat conditions .... in fog and snow ....

John let them reach the door before he called out to her.

"Oh Julie", he said, "Mark is in room 44 on floor 4".

"Pardon", she said, ".... Oh .... Oh yes .... I see ....".

She blushed again.

John smiled.

"Good night Julie", he said.

SIXTEEN

I was up at eight the next morning. In the living room I found breakfast on the side table. Simon must have gone shopping. I'd just poured myself a coffee, when there was a knock on the apartment door. It was Mark.

I poured him a tea.

"Perhaps you should go and wake Julie", I said. "Her room is the fourth door on the right, along the entance hall".

"Oh Julie is taking ....". Then he stopped, realising that he'd walked right into ....

I laughed

"Team bonding is all important on a Mission like this", I said.

"Ain't love grand", he said.

"Spike .... Buffy the Vampire Slayer", I said.

"Amen", said Mark.

*   *   *

John appeared. He poured coffee, took two croissant, and added bacon from the hot dish. He joined us on the sofa.

"I've spoken to Chris Haines", he said. "Chris is busy on the farm this morning, so he suggested we arrive about four o'clock this afternoon. He tells me they can turn Mark into a first century Roman soldier in five days".

"Nigel", he said. "I know that you would like to come up with us, and see Chris again, but I think Julie should join them for the lingustics training. Would you mind staying here to look after The Magdalena for me".

"If Julie, and The Magdalena, are Ok with it, then I'm happy enough", I said.

"Good", said John. "We'd better check that with Julie. I'll knock on her door

103

and ask her to join us".

Mark and I exchanged glances.

"She's just popped out John", I said. "She'll be with us at any moment".

John looked at me, and then cast a thoughtful glance at Mark. He shook his head.

"No rush", he said.

"I should really have a word with my Boss", said Mark.

"I've just finished speaking to him myself", said John. "He asked that you phone him".

Mark realised that he had left his phone in his room. He went off to retrieve it. I wondered if Julie had finished her shower.

*   *   *

By eleven everything had been arranged. Julie had returned to the appartment with Mark. Peter gave them a quizical stare as they came in together .... but he let it go.

The Magdalena was happy for me to look after her, in Julie's absence.

Julie went off to pack, and John and Peter told us they wanted to run tests on equipment at their base. They went off together, John saying he would collect Mark and Julie at one o'clock.

"There's a pub next door", said Mark. "Do you fancy a change of scene".

"I don't drink", I said.

"Neither do I", said Mark.

"We'll have a Coke", I said.

*   *   *

We managed to get the same quiet table that I had shared with Doctor

Samuels, and The Magdalena, two days earlier. I still had the card in my pocket, so I tabbed the drinks.

It was the same barmaid on duty.

"Another friend today", she said, looking longingly at Mark.

"I'm spoken for", he said to her.

"Story of my life ....", she said.

We sat down with the Cokes.

"Well, Fraulein", said Mark, "And what shall we talk about".

I laughed.

"Raiders of the Lost Ark", I said.

Mark nodded .... and sipped his Coke. He was waiting ....

I took a deep breath.

"Mark", I said. "Do you believe there's a God, or do you know there's a God".

He laughed.

"Just check out the barmaid .... could there be a better answer", he said.

We both admired Awesome God's ability with molecular structure.

"Seriously ,Nigel", he said. "There are no atheists on a battle field .... believe me. I've been there".

"And do you think Jesus is The Son of God", I asked.

Mark looked thoughtfully at me.

"And isn't that the million dollar question", he said.

"So what do you think", I asked him.

"Yes", he said, "The evidence is there, if you want to look for it".

"And have you looked", I asked.

"Yes", he said, "I've looked .... and I've found".

We sipped our Cokes thoughtfully, and watched the barmaid polishing tables.

"Game on there .... if you try", said Mark.

I shook my head.

"How are things with Julie", I said.

"Going very nicely thanks", he said

"How are things with The Magdalena", he said.

I narrowed my eyes.

He shook his head .... and laughed.

*   *   *

"I really wasn't expecting that question, yesterday evening, about me being a Catholic", he said.

"We were worried it might be a problem", I said.

"No", he said, "It isn't.....not at all".

"Mark .... Have you ever received Holy Communion".

For the first time since I'd met him, his confidence seemed a little shaken.

"I have", he said, reluctantly.

"In memory .... or the full blown Roman Catholic thing with Transubstantiation", I asked.

"Full blown", he said, even more reluctantly.

"You regret it", I asked.

"Of course I regret it", he said. "The only excuse I can give, is that it was

106

before my History degree, and before my later research".

"So what did you discover to change your mind about it", I asked.

He looked at me thoughtfully.

"I have a feeling I'm not going to tell you anything you don't already know", he said.

"But I'm interested to see if we reached the same place", I said.

"Alright", he said. "But where can you start on it".

"The four Gospels ....", I said.

"Alright then", he said, "Yes .... lets start with the four Gospels".

"And The Last Supper", I said.

He nodded.

"Right", he said, "Let's suppose that this eating bread as Jesus flesh, and drinking wine, as Jesus blood, started at The Last Supper. That's what most people believe .... isn't it".

"If they haven't been told differently", I said.

"So let's look at that more closely", he said. "Four Gospels, but Mark and Luke were not Disciples, so they weren't present at the Last Supper. So their evidence is just hearsay. Are you with me".

"I'm with you", I said.

"Then John", he said. "He was there at The Last Supper, but he doesn't mention the bread and wine incident at all. Not at all".

"So that leaves just Mathew", I said.

"Yes", he said. "That just leaves Mathew .... and he was there. So that's where we should look closely. But was the writer of Mathew's Gospel there, in that upper room, with Jesus, that evening".

"I don't think so", I said.

"Neither do I", he said. "So lets see if we can find an alternative origin for this story. Where else does the idea of eating Jesus' flesh, and drinking His blood, crop up, in the Bible".

"First Corinthians 11:24", I said.

"Yes", he said, "But leave Paul aside for the moment. He never met Jesus, so all his writings are hearsay too".

"John 6:48 to 6:59", I said.

"Right", said Mark. "Now let's look at that in detail. Jesus is speaking in the Synagogue at Capernaum to His Jewish followers, not long before the end".

"Not long", I agreed.

"And it's well and truly time for Jesus to sort the sheep from the goats. Who is going to be bright enough to understand His teachings .... and who is going to be left behind".

"I think I see where you're going", I said.

"Now before we go any further", he said, "You have to understand something very clearly. For the Jewish people Jesus was speaking to, the drinking of any sort of blood was absolutely unthinkable. Totally forbidden. And as for eating human flesh .... it was so far off the forbidden scale, that they hadn't even bothered to write a law about it. Absolutely totally forbidden. Now if you understand that .... and very few people seem to realise it's crucial significance .... we can look at what Jesus says to them in that Synagogue, and work out just where He was coming from. What does He tell them to do Nigel".

"He tells them that if they will have life in them, they must eat His flesh and drink His blood", I said.

"And what do His listeners do when He's told them to do that", Mark asked.

"They all leave Him, apart from The Twelve", I said.

"And it's not very surprising that they react like that", said Mark. "Jesus has just used the most inflammatory metaphor He could possibly choose. He is standing before them, in a Synagogue, of all places, and telling them to eat His flesh, and drink His blood. And doing that .... for the Jewish people .... was absolutely unthinkable. They would have been horrified.

I nodded, looking thoughtfully at this young soldier. We were singing off the same hymn sheet.

"Of course". I said, "He doesn't mean that they should take what He says literally".

Mark laughed .... and shook his head.

"No, of course He doesn't mean it literally. If you read John from about 6:30, you can see that He is likening His body, meaning Himself and His teachings, to the Manna from Heaven. He doesn't mean bite a piece out of My arm on Sunday mornings".

"Or drink a cup of My blood".

"Of course He doesn't", said Mark.

"He means consume the teachings from Heaven. The teachings from His Father. Those teachings are the true bread of life".

I smiled at him.

"Do you know", he said. "There's a really crazy thing about The Holy Bible".

"Which is....", I said.

"It's the all time best selling book", he said, "but it seems to me that it's the all time best selling book that nobody bothers to read".

I laughed

"On the way down here yesterday afternoon", he said, "John was telling me about your take on a rescue attempt being visible in the four Gospels. And you're right. It's there in the four Gospels for all to see .... so why don't they see it. Because they've never actually bothered to read it. That's why".

"So back to Mathew's Gospel", I said.

"Right", said Mark. "Big question .... who wrote first. Was it Bill, or was it Ben. You remember The Flower Pot Men"

"It was Paul .... it was Paul", I said.

"Yes", said Mark, "It was Paul. Paul's writings pre-date the others. So Mathew, Mark, and Luke, got the bread and wine, flesh and blood, thing from Paul. I have to hand it to Luke though. He's obviously not too happy about it, because if you read Luke very carefully .... he doesn't have anybody eating or drinking anything at The Last Supper".

I nodded.

"Again .... you have to read it carefully", I said.

"So we've got Mark, and Luke, taking this incident from Paul in first Corinthians. But where has Paul got it from".

"Probably a verbal account from John, of Jesus teachings in that Synagogue at Capernaum", I said.

"Must be", said Mark. "Chronologically, and story wise, that's the first time the concept crops up".

"So Paul hears about it from any of the Disciples who would actually talk to him", I said, "And that wasn't all of them.......".

"And Paul manages to turn a lovely teaching metaphor into something totally abhorrent to the Jewish faith", said Mark.

"And something that should be totally abhorrent to any civilised society. The consumption of human flesh and blood".

We sat in silence. Mark smiled at me.

"I've always imagined meeting Jesus", he said.

"He'd say to me, "Hi Mark .... so do they remember Me down there".

"And I'd say: "They certainly do Lord".

"And how do they remember Me, Mark", He'd ask.

"Well Lord", I'd say. "They pretend they're eating Your flesh and drinking Your blood on Sunday mornings".

"Well Mark", Jesus would say. "Considering what they did to Me on My last day there …. I'm not too surprised".

Then He might think for a moment.

"Mark", He'd say, "Is everybody eating Me for breakfast on Sunday mornings".

"No Lord", I'd say. "There are some who've seen the Light".

"Mark", He'd say. "I am The Light".

SEVENTEEN

Mark and I stayed in the pub for lunch. The barmaid brought our food.

"Two hot beef sandwiches with chips on the side", she announced.

"And one very sassy barmaid to go", said Mark.

"I'm going", she said.

"Can we persuade John to have her on the team", I said.

"We might persuade John, but you'll never get it by the girls", said Mark.

We tucked in. The barmaid polished tables. Food for the soul.

* * *

We went back to the apartment to meet John at one o'clock. Julie was sitting in the lounge, finishing a salad baguette. She jumped up, crossed the room, and kissed Mark.

"Have you two "come out" then", I said.

"We thought we might as well", said Julie. "Saves us the fee for a room".

"John know yet", I asked.

"I phoned him earlier to tell him", said Julie.

She was fizzing with happiness.

Love's a pretty thing to watch.

* * *

John, Julie, and Mark got away just after one o'clock.

The Magdalena blessed their journey, and she spoke a few words privately to Julie and Mark. I never knew what she said. John had been invited to spend the night at the farm, so he told us he would probably be back for lunch the next day.

Simon appeared to see them off, and gave them canned drinks, sandwiches, and crisps for the journey.

Just after they left, Doctor Samuels arrived to check The Magdalena.

Simon and I were left alone.

"There's fresh coffee in the kitchen", he said.

We went through, sat on stools at the breakfast bar .... a real piece of period design .... and Simon produced home made biscuits. With smarties on the top.

"Your favourite", he said.

I sighed.

"Simon", I said, "Do you know what we're planning".

"Of course I do" he said.

"What's your take on it", I asked.

"Just this", he said. "Suppose you get Him out. What are you going to do with Him then".

I had been wondering this myself

*   *   *

Peter came back to the appartment at about two o'clock. He had lost track of the time, missed lunch, and asked Simon if a sandwich, and soup, might be possible.

Simon went to the kitchen .... and Peter and I sat down.

"Have the others gone off to Hereford yet", he asked.

"They went an hour ago", I said.

Simon came back with a bowl of soup, and a toasted sandwich.

He had brought a pot of tea, and three cups. He sat down with us and we watched Peter eat.

"Peter", I said, "you promised to give me an idea of how your new technology works".

"I did", he said. "Let me finish this, pour me a tea, and we'll do it".

Simon poured three teas.

"Ok" said Peter. "Imagine a room, like this room, but to make it easier, imagine that this room is a perfect cube".

We imagined the room as a perfect cube.

"Right", said Peter. "A square is defined by how many lines".

"Four", said Simon.

"Good", said Peter, "How many lines to define a cube".

"Twelve", I said. "Four at the top, four at the bottom, and the top and bottom squares joined by four vertical lines at the corners".

"Yes", said Peter."Now those twelve lines define a piece of space contained within them. If you define those lines, that is you define their position, length, and direction, you end up with a twelve line "address" for that particular piece of space".

We nodded.

"Now", he said. "That "address" will be unique for every different piece of space you define as a cube".

"Does it have to be a cube", I asked.

"No it doesn't", said Peter, "but you'll see why I chose a cube in a minute".

"So we built two cubes in our workshop, put global positioning sensors on each corner .... that is all eight corners .... and connected the sensors to the computer. We then tried "sending" the twelve line address of cube-one to the "address" of cube-two".

"What happened", I said.

"Absolutely nothing", he said,"Or rather, we thought nothing had happened. Then we realised that we'd sent empty space, and of course, empty space looks like any other piece of empty space, wherever it is".

"Did you put something in the empty space", said Simon.

"Yes we did", said Peter."We put my Teddy bear in cube-one, pressed send, and got the shock of our lives when Teddy appeared in cube-two instantly".

"Instantly", I said.

"Absolutely instantaneous", said Peter. "But this is the really extraordinary part. Because we had sent the piece of space in cube-one to cube-two .... cube-one is now empty. But it's not empty space .... it is empty of space .... it is devoid of space. The space that filled that cube is gone, and it would, in theory, leave a void or a vacuum. But that is not possible, because you cannot have a "space", that is devoid of space".

I looked to Simon. He nodded.

"We're with you so far", I said.

"Ok", said Peter, "Now when the space from cube-one, containing the Teddy bear, moved to cube-two, it pushed the space out of cube-two. You cannot have two pieces of space occupying one piece of space. That's impossible".

"So what happened to the space in cube-two", Simon asked.

"Now that", said Peter, "is the amazing thing. It seems space is like electricity, and it prefers to take the line of least resistance, when it comes to search for a new home. You appreciate that it has to relocate instantly, because you cannot have a piece of space "outside" of space. It has to have a new home.

"Does it move to cube-one", I said.

"Well done", said Peter."It does indeed, but we didn't realise that immediately. We spent a fun afternoon sending Teddy from cube-one to cube-two. But we couldn't find a way to bring him back, other than by picking him up out of cube-two, and putting him back in cube-one".

"Did it effect him in any way", asked Simon.

"We couldn't tell if it was having any physcological effect on him", said Peter, "but physically he remained completely unharmed".

My mind had moved ahead.

"This could have a huge impact on the transport and parcel industries", I said. "Have you thought about the possible implications".

"Oh we certainly have", said Peter, "but it's a very big jump from the Wright brothers making the first powered flight at Kittihawk, to Jumbo jets loaded with three hundred passengers, flying at 30,000 feet".

"So did you get Teddy to travel return", asked Simon.

"We did", said Peter, "but like most of the great discoveries, it was more by accident than design".

Peter looked at his empty tea cup.

"I'll make some fresh", said Simon.

He returned from the kitchen bearing fresh tea, and a new packet of iced finger buns.

"What happened next", I asked.

"We got bored with moving Teddy", he said, "So John went out and bought us a pair of guinea pigs".

"I always thought it was a rough deal, being a guinea pig", said Simon.

"So anyway", said Peter, ignoring him. "We put a guinea pig in cube-one, and encountered our first problem".

"What was that", I said.

"Trying to make the guinea pig stay in the cube", said Peter. "Eventually we solved it by giving him a big piece of carrot. That kept him still".

Simon and I glanced at each other. I thought Simon was looking rather disapproving.

"But with all this faffing about with the guinea pig", said Peter, "we had completely forgotten about Teddy in cube-two. I remembered just a split second too late, having dashed to the keyboard to press send".

"What happened", we said.

"The guinea pig went straight to cube-two", said Peter. "But we had a real surprise when Teddy appeared in cube-one again. Then we had to do some thinking".

Simon passed round the buns.

"Now", said Peter, "It helps if you remember it's the space in the cube we are sending .... not the guinea pig. The space acts as a vehicle for whatever is in that space when we send it.

"But sending the guinea pig in the cube-one space, displaces the space in cube-two", I said. "And that space takes the easiest route to a new home, and jumps to cube-one".

"Exactly", said Peter. "And it takes Teddy with it, because he was in that space".

"Amazing", said Simon, but he still sounded rather disapproving.

"So then we realised", said Peter, "that we didn't have to "send" from cube-two at all. Sending .... we now call it "pushing", because it's easier to think of it in that way. Pushing the space from cube-one to cube-two, means that the space contained in cube-two automatically moves to fill the void in cube-one".

We sat back trying to take all this in.

"But where does the ability to move in time, come into all this", I said.

"At this point in our research", said John, "we had a piece of luck".

"Or a piece of Divine intervention", he added, hastily, seeing my expression.

"John had a family holiday booked …. in Egypt".

"I didn't know he had a family", said Simon.

"Yes" said Peter, "He has a wife and teenage daughters, twins actually …. real characters. One of them works behind the bar, in the pub next door, several times a week".

"Aha", I said.

"Anyway", said Peter. "Off goes John with the family, and I'm not expecting to hear from him for three weeks. Five days later he phones me from Egypt, and he's really excited".

"What about", said Simon.

"He got bored with laying by the pool at the Hotel, and booked himself on an excursion to visit some ancient tombs. His family thought it sounded too boring for words, so he went by himself. They had visited several tombs …. it was a guided tour …. and although John found them interesting …. at the end of the day, he told me, there really wasn't anything to see that he hadn't seen many times on the television".

"But you can see them properly on television", he said, "Because the TV people take big lights inside".

"So John was looking forward to the promise of a cool beer at a bar, when the guide said he had just one more tomb to show them in the same vicinity. It wouldn't take long, he said, because there wasn't much to see, but it was worth a look because it had only recently been discovered.

He took the party to the other side of the wadi …. that's what they call a dry valley, in Egypt …. and led them into a passage, which went about fifty meters, straight into the hillside. At the end of the passage they emerged into a completely empty chamber. The guide shone his light around the walls, which were very smooth, and obviously very accurately cut. The only remarkable feature of the tomb, said the guide, was that it had been measured and found to be a perfect cube. An absolutely perfect cube.

Quite an achievement, when you consider it had been carved from the solid rock.

The party started to file out, heading for that cool beer, but when the guide had shone his torch around the walls, John noticed something.

High up, well out of reach, on the wall to the left of the entrance, were twelve lines of script .... and they didn't look like the normal Egyptian heiroglyphics.

Although the actual symbols were different to ours, they looked remarkably like the twelve line "addresses" for our cubes, as they appear on our computer screens.

John asked if it was Ok to take photographs. The guide said no problem, and then gave him directions to the bar, so he could join the rest of the party when he had finished.

Alone in the "tomb".... if that's what it was .... John took about thirty pictures of the inscription on the wall.

Back at the hotel, John phoned me.

I'd spent the day shuttling guinea pigs back and forth, between the two cubes .... and I have to reassure you", he said hastily, casting a glance at Simon, "that they remained in perfect health, even if I did have to ration their consumption of carrots".

EIGHTEEN

Simon looked at the clock.

"I'd better make a start on the meal for tonight", he said. "Could you two come through to the kitchen, so I can hear how this turns out".

Peter and I followed him through, and established ourselves on the stools at the breakfast bar.

Simon started chopping potatoes.

"We are going English tonight", he said. "My very special potato cake topped shepherds pie, served with spiced gravy".

I wondered how the Magdalena would manage with her fingers.

"Ok", said Peter, "Back to the story. John phoned me from Egypt, and described what he'd found. He emailed all the photographs to me, and although I agreed that the inscriptions appeared identical to our "addresses" .... the symbols were different. I suggested showing them to an expert on ancient texts .... but John wasn't keen. He'd had another idea. If we set up eight of our "Tribbles" in the tomb, it would give us the "address" in modern format. We might then be able to compare, and therefore translate, the ancient version".

"Tribbles". said Simon.

"Oh yes .... sorry", said Peter. "We found the GPS sensors didn't like the slightest breeze, so we put furry covers on them, like the covers you see on outdoor microphones".

"And now they look just like the Tribbles from that episode of Star Trek", I said.

"Spot on", said Peter. "So the next day I found an international courier and sent John eight "Tribbles", and the four telescopic poles to mount them on. They arrived three days later. All John had to do was program his laptop to suit, and we were ready to go.

John asked the hotel to find him a local guide, offering double the going rate, if the man would help carry and set up the equipment. The guide who arrived that evening was an IT student, and his English was very good. He had also worked as an excursion guide, and knew the tombs. He was perfect, and John gave the receptionist at the hotel desk a suitably large tip.

They went at dusk that evening. John asked the guide if there would be any difficulty with security at the site. The guide laughed, and said no .... there was nothing there worth stealing.

They had no problems that evening. John had bought two modern LED lanterns to light the tomb. Helped by the guide, he set up the "Tribbles" on their poles, placing them tightly into the corners of the walls. He blue-toothed the "Tribbles" to the receiver, and connected the receiver to his lap top. He switched on, and a few moments later, he had the twelve line "address" he wanted".

"Did the guide ask him what he was doing", said Simon.

"John told him they were experimenting with new equipment for acurately mapping the tombs", said Peter.

"He also showed the guide the inscription up on the wall, on the off chance that he might be able to read it. He couldn't . He didn't recognise the characters at all.

Back at the hotel, John emailed me the "Addresses" from the "Tribbles". He phoned me later, and gave the name and number of a contact of his, at a code breaking establishment, that do freelance work, mainly for The Govenment.

"John has wonderful contacts", I said.

"He's had a varied career", said Peter.

"The next morning I rang "Steve", as I'll call him. John had already spoken to him. I emailed the photographs of the inscription on the tomb wall to him, and offered to send our modern data as a cross reference. Steve laughed, and said no, because it would be far more fun for his team to decipher the script unaided. I told him we were fairly certain it would decipher as twelve lines of numbers.

An hour later he phoned me back and said, "job done", but he would be interested to check their results against our modern figures. I emailed him the resuts from the "Tribbles".

This time he was on the phone again in twenty minutes. They had a perfect match, he said. Simple rows of numbers. But the inscription in the photographs had one extra digit, spaced a little differently to the rest of the characters.

"Always be careful with spacings", he told me. "Particularly when they occur in ancient texts".

I thanked him, and told him John would settle the bill on his return from Egypt. Steve laughed, and said he owed John several favours. Knock it off the account.

I looked at the translation Steve had sent. We had a perfect match. That was significant because John had predicted that the first and last figures of each line would differ between the script on the walls, and our results. They would differ because the cube our "Tribbles" created was naturally smaller than the rock hewn cube. But we had a perfect match .... and this told us that whoever carved those "addresses" on the wall, must have had equipment similar to ours".

"There's nothing new under the sun", I commented.

"The next day", said Peter, "I set up a cube of the same size as the "tomb" in our workspace, and adjusted the "Tribbles" until I had a perfect size match to the "tomb". It only just fitted under the ceiling, but it would do the job.

John had arranged with me to be back at the tomb at ten-thirty the next evening, and adjusting for the time difference, I put Teddy in my cube, and "pushed" my cube of space to John".

"What happened", said Simon, who was chopping carrots.

"Absolutely nothing at John's end. Teddy disappeared at my end, but didn't arrive with John. I was upset. I'd had Teddy a long time. Of course I only learned the news about Teddy the next day when John phoned me".

"Kharma", said Simon.

"What", said Peter.

"For the guinea pigs", I said.

"Oh right", said Peter looking puzzled.

*   *   *

"We were baffled", said Peter. "It should have worked, but it didn't. It was only when I was looking at my computer data the next day, that I realised what might have happened. I had put both "addresses", the ancient, and the modern, on the same file, not thinking it would matter because of the dead match between them. I had "pushed" my cube to the ancient "address".... but that "address" had an extra digit on each line. I'd sent my "space" somewhere .... but where had I sent it.

So I began to wonder what that extra digit represented.

And suddenly I had one of those great moments ....".

"A Eureka moment", I said.

"Right on", said Peter. "I realised that space itself, just sits there being space until somebody puts something in it. So this piece of space we are sitting in now has always been here, but some years back they built a Premier Travel Inn here. Fifty years ago it was probably occupied by something quite different".

"A hospital", I said.

"Pardon", said Peter.

"A hospital .... there was a hospital here fifty years ago .... there are photographs of it on the wall in the pub next door".

"There you go then", said Peter. "That proves the point. But the real point is that this piece of space was here fifty years ago, just as it is now .... and so I realised that the final digits on the ancient "address" lines might represent a particular point in time for that piece of space".

"Wonder where Teddy is", said Simon, looking concerned.

"Back with me actually", said Peter. "I went back to the workspace and pushed the piece of space in my cube back to the ancient "address" with the extra digits. And Hey presto ....Teddy was back again. Unfortunately he couldn't tell me where he had spent the night.

It seemed most likely to us, that if the final line of digits were, in fact, time points, then they would most likely relate to the time the "tomb" was originally carved".

"And when was that", I said.

"John wasn't really able to find an accurate answer to that", said Peter. He managed to speak to the archeologist who made the discovery, but other than dating it approximately to the period of the adjacent tombs, he couldn't help".

"Do you know now", I asked.

"Yes", said Peter. "We know exactly, because the date is contained in those extra digits, and we eventually managed to extract it".

"So Teddy is Ok, is he", said Simon.

Peter nodded.

"And the guinea pigs are Ok too, are they".

"They're in fine form", said Peter.

"Right", said Simon. "I'm going to throw you out of the kitchen now. I need to get on with some work. I'm going to "push" this shepherds pie into that oven".

We left him to it.

NINETEEN

The next few days became the strangest, and most wonderful time, I had ever experienced.

Peter would disappear off to his workspace as soon as he had finished his breakfast, and we wouldn't see him again, until the early evening.

I was left alone with The Magdalena .... although to say I was left "alone" is a long way from the truth.

We both "opened the doors", and, for me, the constant spiritual companionship was magical. Something I had never experienced before.

My natural "loneliness" was completely banished. Each of us could see the world around us from two different perspectives .... our consciousness of that world was doubled .... and we were both thrilled by the insight that this gave us.

That first morning of those five days together started when I went to wake her for breakfast at 9am. Her ability to sleep for long periods, certainly indicated that She was probably in her late teens. And, of course, She was pregnant.

I knocked on Her door, and called out to Her. The moment She woke, we "connected" to each other, and from that moment, actual physical speech became quite unneccessary.

I returned to the lounge, and she joined me for tea and croissants. We sat opposite each other on the sofas, and we "talked". I have been asked to describe what I mean by "talked", but it is not easy.

Ordinarily we have to use words to communicate our thoughts, and feelings, our wishes, our fears, and our desires .... the list is endless. But when you don't need words to communicate .... what you give, and what you receive, have a clarity that makes ordinary speech seem hopelessly clumsy.

Think of the difference between hearing a sonata on an old crackly 78rpm record, and hearing that same sonata performed live in a concert hall .... and you might begin to understand what communication of this type can feel like.

We sat there for an hour or more, lost in each other.

I discovered that She was happy to be with us, accepting Her absence from Her home, as a neccessary part of the plan.

She knew He was to be crucified .... He had told Her that it was "the cup that he had to drink".

It was something She bore heavily .... She had witnessed crucifixions.

Two nights before, She had brought the cross from under my shirt, to show me that She could accept the symbol for what it was.

We sat .... together.

Eventually, The Magdalena returned to Her room, to spend some time in prayer.

I sat on. Then She invited me to join Her. We prayed.

Doctor Samuels arrived at one o'clock for her normal visit. She was happy that all was well, drank a quick cup of tea with me, and disappeared back to her surgery.

Late in the afternoon, Peter rang to say that John's wife had invited him for dinner. She wanted an update .... and she had a problem with her car. The tail light bulbs weren't working.

That evening Simon joined the Magdalena and I for supper. He had cooked a very simple chicken curry to minimise the amount of time he would have to spend in the kitchen.

It was a very different evening to previous ones.

Despite our attempts to be discreet, Simon soon spotted that the relationship between The Magdalena and myself had changed. If he was curious, he also was discreet, but I suspected that he might want to question me later.

Non the less .... it was a fun evening .... although, as was her habit, The Magdalena left us just before 9pm.

"No good taking that one night clubbing", said Simon.

I rolled my eyes skyward at the thought of taking Mary of Magdala ....
Mary Magdalene .... night clubbing.

"She might love it", laughed Simon.

I helped him carry the dishes through to the kitchen .... and then wished
him a good night.

*   *   *

When The Magdalena joined me the next morning .... I had left her to
wake of her own accord .... I detected a mood of sadness, of longing, in her
demeanour. I had expected a degree of home sickness .... but this was quite
different.

She wanted to go to a Church. She wanted to worship God with others ....
and she longed to be with others, as they worshipped God.

She wanted me to take Her. That presented me with a problem. She was
Jewish.

I conveyed to Her that I would definitely take her to worship with others ....
I would love to do that. But I would have to seek permission from Doctor
Samuels.

And I would have to explain to The Magdalena that we could not go to a
Synagogue.

We spent the morning apart .... in as much as we could ever be "apart". The
Magdalena went off to the kitchen, to show Simon how to make bread ....
the bread She would make at home .... for her family.

I retired to my room to think. I prayed on the problem, and by the time
Doctor Samuels arrived for her normal midday visit, I had a solution.

But I would have to get the doctor's consent first. I explained the situation
to her.

She nodded .... and nodded again .... as Simon offered her a sandwich.

"I thought this might crop up", she said. "The Magdalena is a very devout
young lady .... she would be remarkable in our culture".

"Her boyfriend is The Son of God", I said.

"That would explain it", said the Doctor

"So can we go", I asked.

"I'm Ok with it .... if you're willing to take Her", said the Doctor. " I would have been reluctant if you'd asked me a month ago .... but, to be honest, The Magdalena is so revoltingly healthy, that there isn't a sensible reason for me to say no. And, of course, she is pregnant, and that will have boosted Her immune system".

"So you know about that", I said.

"Nigel", she said, "I am a doctor..............".

"How far along is it", I said.

"Nigel .... Please !!!!!", she said.

"Sorry", I said.

"So where are you going to take Her".

"I'll let you know when I've decided", I said.

*   *   *

That afternoon, I told the Magdalena that we would go to a place of worship on Friday evening.

And then I asked her to sit with me while I explained some stuff to her.

"You know that the man you love will be crucified", I said. "Well as a result of what happens that day, a new "Church" will start. That new "Church" will base itself on the teachings of "Jesus of Nazareth". It will grow to encompass half the world. It will take many forms, and the style of worship will vary enormously from "Church" to "Church", but the love of Jesus will eventually bind them all together.

Tomorrow evening, I am going to take you to my favourite Church .... a Church that is very special to me. Very very special to me".

At dinner that evening .... Simon joined us .... as before. The Magdalena
was animated, and obviously very excited by something. Simon noticed, and
asked me the reason.

"I'm taking Her to Church tomorrow evening", I said.

Simon raised his eyebrows.

"I've got a sister about the same age as the Magdalena", he said. "I don't
think she would be quite that excited if you offered her an evening in
Church as a date".

I laughed.

"You might be surprised", I said. "There will certainly be plenty of young
people at the service tomorrow night".

"Will it be just girls .... or do you get young men as well", asked Simon.

"Plenty of young men there", I said. "Why don't you come with us Simon".

He looked at me thoughtfully.

"Tell you what", he said. "Go with The Magdalena tomorrow .... but I'll
come with you another time .... if you'll take me".

"It would be a pleasure Simon", I said.

"Deal", he said. "Any Church you go to .... it just has to be worth a look".

He thought for a moment.

"Will there be any praying .... like on your knees".

I laughed.

"Simon", I said. "I usually lay on the floor.... it's much more comfortable".

"Yeah .... right", he said.

I smiled. It is more comfortable.

The Magdalena was no less lively the next morning.

She was planning what to wear.

I sat with her over breakfast .... reassuring Her that She would look good in any of the clothes I had seen Her wearing.

She suddenly jumped up and ran to Her room.

She was gone about ten minutes, and I was just beginning to wonder if She was Ok, when She reappeared.

She was wearing the garb of a first century young woman of The Holy Land. The clothes She had arrived in.

I was fascinated .... and I was humbled.

I went, as I had done that first time, and knelt before Her.

And it came home to me .... and perhaps I stopped breathing .... that I was kneeling before Mary Magdalene.

She laughed .... and pulled me up.

She was wearing a long blue dress, deeply cut at the neck, to show the cream shift beneath. She had a matching cream silk sash around Her waist. She wore blue sandals, and a blue scarf, concealing her hair.

I reached out and gently held the soft linen of her gown.

The blue was of an intensity that I had never imagined could be achieved at that time.

She saw I was pleased .... and twirled for me. Girls will be girls.

She was stunning. But She couldn't wear it for Church.

I conveyed to Her that She must wear something more modern.

She dropped Her chin, and pretended to be crestfallen .... but I knew She was only pretending.

She looked up at me , laughed happily, and ran back to her room.

Again .... ten minutes passed.

This time, She had the look for the evening just right.

Blue was Her favourite colour, and She had chosen a "forget-me-not" blue fitted jacket above a knee length lemon cream, pleated skirt. Her blouse, with a demure choke collar was a very pale blue-gray. She had chosen blue gray stockings, and grey court shoes to finish.

Clothes are pretty dull if you are a man. The underwear especially .... is just too dull for words. But if you are a girl ....

I stood .... and admired.

Simon came in. We stood .... and admired.

I haven't described Her yet.

Was She beautiful.

Perhaps not in our modern sense .... no.

Was She pretty then.

Perhaps not in our modern sense .... no.

But She was alive.

Now a daffodil, and a humming bird, are both alive.

But "alive" can mean different things.

Simon and I admired The Magdalena .... and we understood what "alive" can mean.

TWENTY

I took the Magdalena next door to the pub that afternoon. I thought a change of scene would be good, and I knew that they served tea, and toasted tea-cakes .... or danish pastries.

We managed to get the same table.....it was very quiet.

Our "sassy" barmaid was on duty again. She gave us a big smile.

"Can't keep away then", she said.

"No", I said. "It's the sweetness of the staff".

She smiled.

"What can I get you". she asked.

"We would like tea for two please, and two toasted tea cakes with butter".

 I handed her the privilege card.

"I'll bring it all over to you", she said. "Normal table".

"Same one ..... twenty nine", I said.

"Five minutes", she said.

The Magdalena and I sat down.

She gave me a long and thoughtful stare .... and shook Her head .... very gently.

I reached for Her hand .... and made Her a promise.

The tea arrived.

The barmaid placed the tea pot, cups, saucers, milk and sugar, on the table. As she leaned forwards, the pendant on a silver chain around her neck swung into view. It was a stylish capital letter T.

"What does the letter T stand for", I asked. .

"T for Tara", she said.

"I thought it might be T for trouble", I said.

I pulled my own pendant into view. I kept the top part covered with my thumb.

"I've got one too", I said.

"What does yours stand for", she asked.

I took my thumb away.

She looked thoughtfully at the cross. She looked at us both.

"I know what it stands for", she said.

"What", I said.

"T for trouble", she said. "I'll fetch your teacakes".

* * *

I'll have to admit I was looking forward to the evening very much.

That Friday was the third Friday of the month .... and at The Destiny Centre .... the third Friday of every month is "A Night with The King".

"The Destiny Centre" is everything that a Church should be.

Founded ten years ago by it's leaders, Pastors John Paul Oddoye, and his wife Abigail .... the congregation was originally based amongst the black African community in the City. But their Church had grown, and if the African style of worship was, perhaps, something of a shock, if you grew up with Church of England, you soon put this aside, as you came to enjoy being amongst people who actually KNEW there was a God, people who lived with God in their lives at every moment, and people who put everything into worshipping that God. I loved them all.

Yes .... I was nervous when I went to my first service there. I was nervous because I'm white. But nobody there seemed to notice. I was there in The House of God .... and that's what mattered to them. And they mattered to me .... and they always will.

Because "Night with The King" only happens once a month, it is seen as an "Event", and people like to dress up for it. It's a smart evening .... which is why I was happy that The Magdalena had caught the mood.

Now there are some people who think its fine to go to Church in a T shirt and shorts .... and I'm not critical in any way, because the important thing is that they want to go to Church .... and they are there in Church. But for me .... just personally .... I like to make an effort.

I like to get myself into the mood for Church .... into the zone .... as it were. So I shower, and I relax, and I dress in my "Best clothes".... meaning clothes I wouldn't wear for work, because I wouldn't want to get them dirty. On Sundays .... yes .... I will often wear a suit. But for tonight .... I chose a pale grey blazer over a turquoise shirt, with black trousers and shoes. I love the pale grey jacket. Very smart.

At six-thirty The Magdalena and I stood in the living room dressed for action. Simon had offered to drive us there.

He nodded approvingly at our appearance.

"No tie, Nigel ....", he said to me.

I pointed to the cross at my throat

"Ok", he said. "Lets motor".

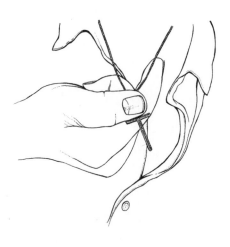

TWENTY ONE

John arrived back at the apartment, with Mark, and Julie, a little after 1pm. Simon had timed lunch for one fifteen, and to celebrate their return .... he had layed out a picnic meal, on a folding table which he had set up in the living room.

We were all pleased to see them back. The Magdalena talked rapidly, and delightedly, to Julie, about Her night in Church, and Julie, in return, had a lot of fun describing Mark's training as a Roman soldier.

Peter arrived just in time. He spotted the picnic.

"This is a good idea", he said. "Thanks for doing this Simon .... it's really different".

On a chequered blanket, Simon had layed out sandwiches, and crisps, and scotch eggs, and sausage rolls, breaded chicken pieces, tiny pasties, and baby tomatoes. There were bottles of lemonade, and ginger beer, and a flask of coffee. Cups, plates, and knives and forks were all plastic, as they should be for a picnic.

"Well this is a novelty", said Doctor Samuels, who arrived in time to capture the last scotch egg.

Simon had created an atmosphere of light hearted fun .... and we all appreciated his efforts. Everybody chatted away "ninety to the dozen", as my grandmother would have said, and for a while, any tensions we had about the forthcoming events were put aside.

We finally subsided onto the sofas, Simon came round with fresh tea, and we looked to John, who was obviously preparing to move things on to the next stage.

"Ok", he said. "We are all back together. We now have our Roman soldier. Peter tells me he is happy with the technical side of things. Doctor Samuels tells me that The Magdalena, and Nigel, are in perfect health, and this evening I would like to run through the final plan, and make sure everybody knows what they are doing, and when they are doing it.

I suggest we relax this afternoon .... Mark, Julie, and I, have certainly had a hectic few days .... but I would like us all to be here together for six o'clock. We'll break for our evening meal at seven thirty, and hopefully wrap things up afterwards. Are you all Ok with that".

We all nodded our assent. Mark and Julie disappeared together, Doctor Samuels went off with The Magdalena, John went to his room, and Peter and I were left with the last of the tea. We could hear Simon in the Kitchen.

Peter stretched, yawned, and lay back on the sofa.

"We are good to launch", he said.

"When are we going", I said.

"That's up to John", he said, "but I know he prefers sooner rather than later .... and we can't keep Mark for too much longer".

"Well", I said, "I might as well go and have a lay down .... as it looks like we might go on for quite a while this evening".

"Sounds good", said Peter, "See you later".

As I headed from the room, Peter pulled his laptop from it's case. It was a deliciously expensive lap top.

"Peter", I said, turning back to him.

"You spend a lot of time on that lap top. Do you have other business interests, apart from time travel".

He laughed.

"I do Nigel", he said, "I'm a major share holder in a well known hotel chain .... and in theory.... I do have a job title in their organisation".

"Let me guess", I said. "Is it Area Manager, Northern Europe, by any chance".

He laughed.

"Well done Nigel", he said. "You got there in the end".

"See you at six", I said.

He opened his laptop .... and smiled.

*   *   *

I joined the others in the living room just before six. Everybody was there, apart from The Magdalena.

Peter had set up a screen, with a projector connected to his laptop, on the coffee table.

"Ok", said John, looking round. " We are all here, except for The Magdalena. There's no point in causing her any unneccessary distress with this first part, but She'll join us for dinner .... by which time we should be on more cheerful ground. Peter is going to kick off for us.

"My part is relatively simple", he said. "We have our cube of space defined by the "Tribbles", set up at our base .... our workspace. The team will change into first century clothing. John and Julie have organised that .... and each person will be responsible for organising whatever equipment they need to take. Medical gear for Doctor Samuels, uniform and weapons for Mark, etc. I suggest you all make check lists.

Nigel .... there will be some tools for you to acquire .... but we'll get to that later.

When everything is good to go, you take your places inside the cube, tuck your fingers and toes in, I press "send". Hey presto .... you're all there in the first century Holy Land".

"So will there be any sensation of travel", I asked.

"Ask Julie", said Peter, "She's done the trip twice".

I turned to Julie.

"No", said Julie, "There's no particular sensation that I noticed. You just feel your feet drop two inches to the ground".

141

I looked back to Peter.

"You have to stand on something inside the cube", said Peter. "We've found that a mound of sand works best".

"Why", I asked.

"Because the bottom plane of the cube of space we are going to "send" is a couple of inches off the floor", said Peter. "If you actually stood on the floor .... you would arrive without the bottom two inches of your feet. Remember .... we can only send the space contained within the cube".

"Ah", I said, "You weren't joking about tucking your fingers and toes in then".

"No", said Peter.

"Another question", I said.

"Go for it", said Peter.

"Where will we actually be when we get there".

"About a mile outside Bethany, putting you about two miles from Jerusalem". said Peter.

"John made a site visit .... in modern times, I mean .... a few weeks ago .... and found the perfect spot. An area of flat rock .... far enough from the village to be safe of development. There was every indication that the spot was identical in appearance two thousand years ago. It was perfect for what we wanted".

"And are the "Tribbles" still there then", I asked.

"Nope", said Peter, "John set them up and recorded the GPS data on his computer .... but once we have those co-ordinates .... we can "push" to them without the "Tribbles" being needed again. It took us a while to realise that the second set aren't neccessary once you have the data for that piece of space."

"So you needn't have set up the "Tribbles" in that rock "tomb" in Egypt", I said.

"No", said Peter, "We could have just taken the "address" off the wall .... but remember our modern data helped confirm that the inscription was what we thought it might be".

"I'm with you", I said.

I thought for a moment ....

"Peter", I said, "What happens if a camel, or a goat , or something, wanders into that space outside Bethany at the wrong moment".

"Or a person", said Julie.

"They'll find themselves in our workspace in our time", said Peter. "That piece of space swaps places with our piece of space, remember".

"I hope they tuck their fingers and toes in", said the Doctor.

"Or their hooves", said Julie.

We pondered on hoofless first century goats in Peter and John's workspace.

"Ok", said Peter. "Lets move things on. From the moment you find yourselves on that spot outside Bethany, in the first century .... Mark takes command of the team".

"I'll just intervene here, Peter, if I may", said John. "You all know that Mark has training and experience of working "behind enemy lines", and although there is no particular reason that any of you will be in any real danger .... I think Mark's experience will be worth a lot "in the field", as it were. Anybody have any feelings on the matter .... speak now, etc .....".

"I'm quite happy for Mark to direct us", I said.

The others nodded their agreement.

"Ok", said Peter, "If we're all happy .... I'll hand over to Mark. Captain Rossi .... if you're ready".

"Always ready", said Mark.

He sat up a little straighter, and visibly took command of the team.

"Right", he said. "So there we are standing in the middle of nowhere .... five people, with various bags and bundles. It isn't quite the problem it would normally be for me and a platoon, because we'll be in period costume .... and because we are arriving in the run-up to The Feast of the Passover in Jerusalem. There will be lots of strangers about, travelling to the city. With a bit of luck, we shouldn't draw too much attention to ourselves".

"How far away in days will the Passover be", asked Julie.

Mark smiled at her.

"We are aiming at a point just two days before", he said. "That's the point The Magdalena was lifted from .... and the point John and Peter want to return Her to".

"It's not absolutely crucial to hit that point exactly", said John, "but we are worried about the possible consequences if we have The Magdalena missing from her own time for any extended period".

"And from my point of view, and speaking from my training and experience", said Mark, "the less time we spend in the field of operations .... the less chance there is for something to go wrong".

"Agreed .... absolutely", said John.

"So", said Mark. "As always, the first thing we need to do is to secure the exit . We'll mark the corners of the transfer location, and build a platform of sand, or stones, whatever, to stand on for return trip. Once we've done that, we need local information, so while we shovel sand, the Magdalena will walk to her home, to find out just where we are time-wise".

"What will we do while she's gone", I asked.

"I'm hoping She'll only be gone a couple of hours, at the most", said Mark. "The plan is nothing more complicated than finding a tree to sit under, and then having a snack. Again .... with so many strangers travelling to Jerusalem, for The Passover, we shouldn't look out of place".

"What if somebody does come along", asked Doctor Samuels.

"Julie speaks Aramaic", said Mark, "so she should be able to fend them off".

"What happens then", said Julie.

Mark took a breath.

"That depends entirely on the information The Magdalena brings back for us", he said. "But the most likely scenario is that The Magdalena takes us to her home. It's likely to be quiet, virtually empty, because her family will have gone to Jerusalem, again for The Passover, but even if her family are there, it won't be a problem. She will explain that we are friends of Jesus .... and we shall be welcomed".

"I would like to have met Lazarus and Martha", I said.

"And you might", said Mark, "but my priority is the operation .... to get Him out".

"And then ....", said Doctor Samuels.

"We wait for information again", said Mark. "And this time it's the Disciple Peter that we are waiting on.

Joseph of Aramathea takes Peter into the precincts of Pilates court, so he can keep up with what's happening. When he knows the outcome, he can return to the other Disciples with an update".

"Peter gets a bit of a rough deal at this point", I said.

"I know", said Mark. "I've been in his situation myself.

He gets spotted and has to deny he knows Jesus. But he wasn't a coward. He had the responsibility of returning with news to the others. A big responsibility .... so he has to deny Jesus .... he hasn't any option. People take that "When the cock crows, thou shalt deny me thrice", business far too seriously. Jesus liked to tease Peter. Look at the "walking on water" challenge he gave him. Jesus knew he'd sink".

"How will we get Peter's news", asked Julie.

"Peter will go back to the Disciples. The Magdalena will be with them. She'll come to us to tell us the crucifixion is imminent. The team will then split. The Magdalena will take us all to the new tomb in the garden near the place of execution. Once Julie, and Doctor Samuels, are safely inside, She'll show Nigel and I the likely position of the cross. It's a regular place for crucifixions, so there won't be much doubt about the location .... and in any case we know it has to be near that new tomb.

Nigel and I will make what plans we can, based on what we find, and The Magdalena will return to the Disciples.

We know that She will be at the crucifixion with Jesus' mother Mary, and with "the Disciple that Jesus loved" .... which is usually taken to mean John".

"I'm not so sure about that", I said.

"Who do you think it might have been", said Doctor Samuels.

"Mark", I said.

"I'd like to hear your reasons for that idea", said Mark.

"Perhaps give you something to chat about while you're waiting for The Magdalena", said John.

"It's a date", I said.

TWENTY TWO

"So", said Mark, "Things get very unpleasant from here on. Nigel and I get to watch the crucifixion of Jesus of Nazareth …. and that's not something I'm looking forward to.

For Nigel …. it's much worse. He'll explain why in a minute …. but I'll wind up my part, at a suitable moment, and if there isn't a suitable moment …. I'll have to make one …. I remove the relevant soldier from the equation, substitute myself, and do the non lethal spear thrust.

Then I'll stay on guard, until Joseph, Nicodemus, and Nigel arrive. I'll help them remove Jesus from the cross, and get Him into the tomb. The Doctor takes over inside. I'll stand guard outside.

"Don't forget that Pilate authorises a guard for the tomb", I said.

"I hope we'll be long gone by the time he's organised that", said Mark.

"Nigel …. over to you".

I looked round at them all thoughtfully.

"I'm here", I said, "because of a certain "gift" I have.

I discovered this gift …. or rather …. I realised I had it …. the day I started school".

"I'll intervene again", said John. It's probably best if I tell them, Nigel".

I agreed.

"Nigel is empathic", said John. "Empathic to an extra-ordinary degree.

Doctor Samuels and I believe that his ability to "connect" to another person …. in this case Jesus Himself …. will be a great help in getting a successful outcome to this operation. We want to get Jesus off the cross alive. We want to treat His wounds, and get Him back to full health. And finally, we want to place to Him where His teachings can continue".

The others looked back to me.

"I promise I'm not reading your minds now", I said. "I can turn it off to a great degree".

They laughed.

"I'll certainly do all I can", I said, "but I'm concerned about "connecting" to somebody who is going to undergo the crucifixion process. I might not be strong enough to maintain the link to someone enduring that degree of pain and trauma. Doctor Samuels will tell you what we have to deal with".

* * *

Doctor Samuels stood, and asked Peter to turn on the projector.

"Image number one please, Peter", she said.

The screen faltered for a moment, then filled with one of the most famous images in the world. The face of Jesus, from the Turin Shroud.

"Ok" said the Doctor, "You'll all recognise this as The Turin Shroud".

Peter panned out, until we had the entire front body image of the shroud.

Doctor Samuels looked at me and narrowed her eyes.

"Nigel", she said, "Are you sure The Magdalena isn't going to get any of this. I really would rather that we spare her the next half hour".

"I'm switched right off", I said. "I promise".

She continued to look searchingly at me .... and eventually .... deciding she was convinced .... she turned back to the screen.

"Crucifixion, as used by the Romans at this period", she said, "is still considered by those who have studied the subject, to be the most brutal, cruel, and sadistic means of execution ever devised. If we are going to bring this rescue attempt to a successful conclusion, you'll all need to know what we'll be dealing with.

Whether this really is the burial shroud of Jesus of Nazareth .... we'll probably never know for certain. But whether or not it is Jesus, there's no doubt that it is the image of a crucifixion victim. I personally think that it is the real thing .... but that's a discussion for another time".

"Why do you think it is Jesus", said Julie.

"Julie", said John. "That really is a huge subject .... and we need to press on".

"Sorry", said Julie.

"I'll lend you Ian Wilson's book about The Shroud, Julie", I said.

"Anyway ....", said Doctor Samuels. "This might be Jesus, or it might not be, but the image does give us a lot of useful information.

She asked Peter to show the reverse.

"What are all those marks, like little dumb bells, all over the back", said Julie.

"Those are the marks left by the flogging", said Doctor Samuels. "The whip called a flagrum, had two thongs, tipped with lead weights. Those weights cause the marks.

This lead weighted version of the flagrum was the new improved model. There was an earlier version where the thongs were tipped with razor sharp sheep bones. Those bone tips would tear away flesh and muscle right down to the rib cage. After forty lashes with the bone tipped flagrum, the physical damage to the torso was so severe, that victims were unlikely to make it to the cross alive.

In fact.... there is a theory that the cross may originally have been simply the means of displaying the body of the flogged victim to the population".

"And then the Romans found it was much more fun to nail people to a cross while they were still alive", I said.

"Yes", said the Doctor. "The Romans practised crucifixion over a long period .... and by the time they got to Jesus, they had perfected the art. It was cruelty almost beyond modern comprehension.

The lead tipped flagrum pulverises the flesh where it strikes", she said. "Several strikes on the same spot will tear through the skin. As the lead tips whip around the body, they bruise the ribs, and a blow to the face will smash out teeth, and rip out eyes. But the objective wasn't to kill. The flogging was designed to cause the maximum amount of pain and shock trauma, whilst still leaving the victim alive to endure the cross.

Following the flogging, which was limited by law to forty lashes, meaning eighty impacts by the lead tips, the victim was expected to carry the cross bar of his cross to the place of execution. Most were too weakened by dehydration, and blood loss, to carry their cross bar very far.

"Simon of Cyrene", was forced to help Jesus", I said.

"So at this point", said Doctor Samuels, "Jesus will be severly weakened. He will already be suffering from the effects of dehydration .... and He will be suffering from shock. Nigel and Mark will both have seen the very peculiar effects that shock can have".

"John's Gospel has Jesus back in front of Pilate, after the flogging", I said.

"I've always thought that John was using some artistic licence there", said the Doctor. "Pilate wouldn't want to look at a flogged Jesus. Not good for his dignity at all. Not to mention the blood all over the floor. No .... it's most likely that Jesus was taken to be executed straight after the flogging".

"I tend to agree with you", I said. "It doesn't feel like Pilate's style at all".

When the soldiers, usually four of them, reach the place of crucifixion, they will nail the cross bar to the vertical post, which, at this point is laying on the ground. Then they will push Jesus down onto His back, stretch His arms along the cross piece, and hammer the iron nails through His wrists. Peter .... image three please".

We were looking at the lower arms, and hands, of the figure on the shroud.

"You'll notice that the nails go through the wrists, just above the hands", said the Doctor. "Two reasons: First, the soft tissue of the palms can't possibly support the weight of a grown man. Secondly, there is a nerve centre at that point in the wrist. Driving the nail through that point causes acute distress, because it destroys the nerve centre, and causes numbness in the arms, nausea, and sometimes vomiting .... adding to the dehydration problem".

"Did the Romans know that the nerve centre was there in the wrist", said Julie.

"They certainly did", said the Doctor. "That's why they liked to use nails when they could have lashed the wrists to the cross with cords .... Image four please Peter

The soldiers will then bring Jesus' knees upwards about nine inches, place the left foot over the right, and drive the biggest nail .... more of a spike .... through both feet. We know He refused the pain reliever when He was offered it.

They say Jesus didn't scream on the cross. I don't believe them.

Jesus can still breath properly at the moment. He is laying on his back, nailed to the cross.

The bottom two feet of the vertical post is squared off, and fits between two stone slabs set vertically in the ground to create a slot. The three soldiers push the cross to the upright position. there is sufficient back and forth room in the slot to allow them to use wooden wedges to put the cross properly vertical, to tilt it a little forwards, or to tilt it a little backwards. Tilted backwards a little, some of the victims weight is taken by the upright, but the wounds on the back, from the flogging, will rub against the post. Tilted forwards, the man will hang forwards from the nails, causing agonising pain in the shoulder joints.

But from the moment that cross reaches the vertical position Jesus will begin to have difficulty with His breathing. He can breath in ..... but the only way He can exhale is to take the strain off His chest muscles by pushing Himself upwards with his legs.

Thats why the knees were pushed upwards. For Jesus to exhale, He must try to straighten His legs. He must push His torso up the cross, allowing His chest muscles to relax. Remember that His whole body weight is hanging on three iron nails. The one through the feet also goes through a nerve centre, and if the Roman soldiers got it just right, that spike through the feet, through the nerve centres there, would cause spasmic upward jerking of the legs.

Every breath Jesus takes now, will cause Him excruciating agony. That's the cruel thing about crucifixion. It takes something we all do every day, without even thinking about it .... breathing .... and turns it into repetitive, searing, and agonising pain.

This is the part of crucifixion that the Romans thought was great fun to watch. The victim pushes up, trying to exhale, and then drops down again .... like a puppet. For the best entertainment they would crucify three or four victims in a line, and watch them bob up and down, screaming in agony as they did so. And all the time the entire body weight is suspended on those three spikes through the nerve centres, in the wrists and feet.

But it gets worse. Because Jesus can't exhale properly, carbon dioxide will begin to build up in His muscles. And the muscles will begin to knot and cramp. If you have had cramp when swimming, then you'll have experienced the tiniest part of what Jesus will suffer. He has no way to relieve the cramp. He must endure it.

Every breath He takes results in pain beyond our imagination. And then the despair starts, as He realises that the only possible end to this distress and agony is death. Despair was a recognised part of the crucifixion process. The Romans knew all about it".

"My God, My God. Why hast Thou forsaken Me". I said.

Everybody had gone very quiet. Julie stood, visibly upset.

"I need a few minutes", she said. She went from the room.

Mark looked after her.

"Perhaps I'd better ....", he said.

We nodded. He hurried after Julie.

Doctor Samuels watched them go. She nodded.

"I'll finish", she said.

"The most extraordinary thing about all this, is that it is so misunderstood. You hear about Jesus sacrificing His blood on the cross. But it's not really accurate to say that.

Yes, the puncture wounds in the wrists and feet would bleed, but not enough to kill you. There is no single part of the crucifixion process that actually causes death. Some victims survived a week on the cross, before they succumbed to exhaustion, asphixiation, dehydration, blood poisoning, or possibly heart failure.

The Roman ideal was to keep the victim alive on the cross, in agony, for as long as possible. Three days was the average time for a victim to die".

"Unless the legs were broken", I said.

"Yes", said the Doctor. "The Roman soldiers would accept bribes to smash the femurs with an iron bar. Once the lower legs were broken, the victim could no longer push upwards, and raise his chest to exhale. Suffocation was fairly rapid.

There is only one historical account of somebody surviving crucifixion. He was taken down from the cross with two others. All three of them had medical care .... but even then .... two of them died".

* * *

"Now", she said, "We do have some things in our favour.

If the shroud image is in fact Jesus, and there are good reasons to suppose it is, then the evidence is that the flogging He received was not quite as severe as it could have been. Possibly, His uncle Joseph had bribed the soldiers to hold back a little. There are several accounts of Jesus speaking from the cross, and that also points to His still retaining some strength.

And finally .... and this is the most important point .... He is only on the cross for six hours. Spare Him that fatal spear thrust, and I am very confident that we can save Him.

I need a living Jesus, in that tomb, as quickly as you can get Him to me.

I'll have seen far worse after a car crash .... believe me".

Mark came back into the room.

"She'll be Ok in a minute", he said. "You didn't pull any punches with that ....".

"Sorry", said Doctor Samuels. "Very few people seem to have any real knowledge of what a crucifixion entails".

"One question", said Mark. "You always imagine the cross as being quite high up. How far off the ground would a victim be".

"That's a good question", said Doctor Samuels. "For the executioners to break the legs .... one imagines the lower legs of the crucified man being about a meter, or a meter and a half, from the ground. But The Magdalena told Julie that she saw a crucifixion where the victim's toes were barely clear of the ground .... so his family could literally look him in the face as he died.

Once you are nailed to the cross .... it really doesn't matter how far off the ground you are. The end will be the same".

"They had to attach the sponge from which Jesus drank, to a reed", I reminded them.

"That again indicates the victim being well up off the ground", said the Doctor.

"The height they could achieve would depend, to some degree, on how secure they could make the base of the cross", said Mark.

"True", said the Doctor. "But however high He is .... you have to get Him down as gently as possible. Remember His whole body weight is held on those three nails".

We fell silent.

"We've many reasons to be positive", said Doctor Samuels. "Give Him to me alive .... and I'll keep Him that way. I promise you".

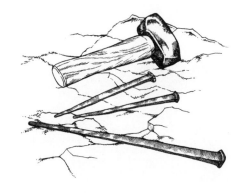

TWENTY THREE

We broke for our evening meal at this point. Mark and Julie returned, Julie obviously having done that wonderful and mysteriously feminine thing known as "freshening up".

She went to fetch The Magdalena, Simon appeared to announce supper, and we all went through to a roast beef dinner .... with seared mediterranean vegetables, of course.

The Doctor had left us all a little shaken. I had already known most of what she had described, but her brutal un-sentimental treatment of the subject had made me realise what I might encounter .... if I could make that "connection" that she wanted.

We went straight in on the main course that evening, and as we ate, the Doctor explained that her priority in the tomb would be stabilising her patient, and carrying out initial first aid to the wounds.

"There shoudn't be anything I can't help Him with", she said. "Once I'm happy that He is stable, I hope we can get Him back to my facility here .... but it's over to Peter to tell you how that will be managed".

Peter nodded.

"John and I have spent a lot of time on this", he said. "As you know we have just three days .....".

"Just like Time Team .....", said Julie.

"Yes Julie, just like Time Team", said Peter, "But with the difference that our piece of "history" is still happening".

"So we looked at setting up a space cube in the tomb, using the "Tribbles", said John.

"Trouble is", said Peter that there are just too many things to go wrong. We haven't found a way for our equipment to transmit the initial "addresses", of safe empty space, through time yet".

"So somebody would have to return to the cube near Bethany, and make the return trip here with the data", said Mark.

"Exactly", said Peter. "And while they are doing that .... they might as well bring Jesus with them".

"How far would we have to carry our patient", asked Mark.

"About two miles", said John, "depending on the site of the tomb".

"Yeah", said Mark, thoughtfully, "That's not too bad with five of us. We can share the carrying. We can do it".

"But how are you going to know when to bring us back", I said.

"Well", said Peter, "We don't "bring you back" as such. We "push" the space in the cube at our end, to your cube. You come back to us, as the space in your cube moves to fill our void. We intend to make that "push" on the hour .... every hour .... until we have you back".

"When will you start to do that", asked Mark.

"We think it's best to start doing it one hour after your initial trip", said John. "So you'll have a service to rely on from the start".

"Sounds good", said Mark, "but we'll have to be very careful to stay clear of our cube until we want to return".

"Very clear", said Julie. "Remember the fingers and toes thing".

"We want to get you all back in two "pushes" said John. "Doctor Samuels, her Patient, and The Magdalena first. Then Julie, Nigel, and Mark. With an extra person, and He"ll almost certainly not be able to stand, there simply won't be enough room in the cube to fetch you all in one go".

We nodded our understanding.

"And what happens when we have all got back, and Jesus is here with us", asked Julie.

"Doctor Samuels, Nigel, and the Magdalena have three days to get Jesus as fit, and well, and mobile, as possible", said John. "Then He and The

Magdalena will return to Bethany. Jesus has some appearances to make. Following those .... well, that's up to Him and The Magdalena. There are various possibilities".

"Languedoc area of France .... Kashmir in India ....", I said.

"Various possibilities", said John, in a tone that told me to wait.

It seemed that we had taken our plans as far as was possible, for the moment.

The Magdalena had perceived that there was an air of great confidence around the table.

She spoke to Julie.

Eventually Julie turned to us.

"The Magdalena wants you all stand and bow your heads in prayer", she said. "She wishes to call the blessing of The One True God upon our enterprise, that His Son will be able to continue His Ministry of peace and love and understanding".

We stood .... and bowed our heads.

The Magdalena spoke. The musical quality of Her native Aramaic, combined with Her sincerity, made it totally unnecessary for Julie to translate. It was a prayer that we all felt, as much as heard.

She finished.

I looked up. She was crying. Julie put an arm around Her shoulders, and gently led Her from the room.

We sat in silence. I think the prayer had brought home to us the implications of what we were about to attempt.

"So when do we go", I said.

John looked to Doctor Samuels.

"Are we fit Doctor", he asked.

"Fit to go .... anytime", she replied.

"Peter", he asked.

"I'm ready", said Peter.

"Nigel .... how about you", said John.

I paused .... looking at him, and Peter.

"I could have thrown you both out that afternoon", I said.

"Are you wishing you had", said John.

"I've met Mary Magdalene", I said. "What do you think .... if things are ready .... yes I'm good to go".

"Up to Mark then", said John.

We looked to the soldier.

"We'll go tomorrow afternoon then", said Mark, "Let's get the job done. Let's get Him out".

The dinner party broke up. Mark, John, and Peter, headed for their rooms.

The Doctor and I sat on.

"Doctor Samuels .... you have something you want to say to me", I prompted.

She looked at me.

"How on earth did you .... Oh sorry", she said, "Silly question really".

"What is it", I asked.

"We are all assuming He died because of the spear thrust", she said. "Suppose He didn't. Suppose He dies of Despair".

"Can somebody die of despair", I asked.

"Oh yes", she said. "You can die of despair ....

Nigel ..... That's where you come in .... don't allow Him to go that way".

TWENTY FOUR

"Where are Mark and Julie", I asked Peter.

"Gone swimming together. They got up early, and did a five mile run, and now they've gone to the pool.

 Mark has to keep very fit .... and Julie's pretty fit already".

"They're getting on well", I said smiling.

"Very well", said Peter, not looking up from his laptop.

"Which pool have they gone to", I asked.

"The one in the basement", said Peter.

I stared at him.

"There's a swimming pool in the basement".

"There is", said Peter.

"I never new Premier Travel Inns had a pool in the basement", I said.

"It's not the Hotel pool", said Peter. "It's a private pool for this apartment".

I considered this.

"Peter", I said. "You told me this apartment belongs to the area manager".

"It does", said Peter.

"How big is his area", I said.

"Northern Europe", said Peter.

"Ah", I said.

I checked the coffee pot. It was empty.

"Peter", I said. "You didn't mention the pool to me".

"Nigel", he said. "You haven't been to a swimming pool since you learned to surf".

I shook my head in disbelief.

"I've been down to the pool myself, this morning", he said. "Surf's not up".

"Is there anything you haven't researched about me".

"Not much", he said, still absorbed in his screen.

"Do you know my passwords", I asked.

He looked up from his laptop, rolled his eyes skywards, and went back to the screen.

I took that as a yes ....

*   *   *

Lunch that day was a quiet affair. Although the whole team was there .... everybody seemed pre-occupied with their own thoughts.

I'd been out that morning with Mark. We went to a tool shop, and bought a good hacksaw, and ten spare blades, to deal with the nails. I wasn't expecting any problems with cutting through the relatively soft iron that they used then. We also purchased a crow bar, a short hafted sledge hammer, and a bow saw for wood, in case we had trouble lowering the cross. Again with plenty of spare blades.

We bundled our gear .... my tools, and Marks uniform and equipment into several course woven woolen blankets.

Mark showed me what the Ermine Street Guard's armourer had done to his spear .... the pilum.

Seeing that it was too long for ease of transport, he had sawn the shaft into two halves. He had then fitted brass screw threads into the two pieces. When assembled, the joint was all but invisible. He had also sharpened the cutting edges of the spear head. The spear would create a convincing wound with very little effort.

Doctor Samuels had brought very little in the way of equipment. I commented that I expected to see her with all sorts of gear.

"I've got four major wounds to treat", she said, "Various minor wounds, and, of course, the shock trauma to deal with. Bandages, swabs, and a selection of hypodermics will see me through, until we get Him into my surgery".

Julie, as translator, had little more than some personal effects to carry, so she would help Mark with his gear.

Peter had hired a small van that morning, and just after lunch he took all the bundles we had heaped up in the hallway of the apartment, and moved them to the "Departure lounge" .... as he and Mark had started to call it.

He returned at 2pm. We said goodbye to Simon.

The ladies travelled in the car with John and Mark.

Peter and I followed in the van.

Our destination, when we reached it some thirty minutes later, was a remarkably shabby looking building, on a rather run down industrial estate. We drove to the rear of the unit. I looked at the faded and peeling paint on the doors and windows, the weeds in the car park .... and began to wonder.

Peter must have sensed my puzzlement.

"Wait till you see inside", he said.

He used a Yale key to unlock the door, and pushed it open. It stuck a little. He went to an alarm system control panel on the left wall, pressed his palm onto a screen, and tapped in a code on the key pad that had appeared. A recorded voice greeted him personally, and asked him to say his name clearly.

"That system wasn't cheap", said Mark, who had watched with interest.

"It wasn't", said John.

Through the second door .... I heard the lock release .... things were very different to the outside.

Polished floors, immaculately painted walls, expensive light fittings. No expense spared.

"External appearances can be deceptive", said Peter.

He ushered us through a third door, into what was obviously their centre of operations.

If we'd imagined the sort of laboratory set ups you see in the movies .... well, we were disappointed. True .... there were several computer screens on desks, and shelves of various equipment, but there really wasn't that much to see.

"We try and keep things tidy", said Peter.

The most noticable thing in the room was the set up in the centre. Four black poles on stands, stretching nearly to the ceiling, marked the corners of a four metre by four metre square. Between the poles, on the floor, a platform of sand, about six inches high, had been carefully built up and levelled smooth.

Attached to the top and bottom of each pole were what appeared to be fluffy tennis balls. The "Tribbles".

I had just stepped forward to take a closer look at my first "Tribble", when there was a cry of delight from Julie. She had spotted the guinea pigs, in their cage, against the far wall. The girls all went to admire the guinea pigs.

Peter turned to us smiling.

"I'll show Nigel and Mark to their changing room", he said.

The girls didn't appear to hear him.

We followed him back through the workspace doors, turned left along a corridor, and were shown into a room that was decorated as a bed sitting room.

"Bathroom through here", said Peter, opening a door. "Your clothes are on the beds. Nigel you're there .... Mark .... over there".

He pointed to the two beds. Each had a neatly folded pile of clothing .... ready to wear.

"I'll leave you to change", he said. "I'll show the ladies to their room. Come back to the main room when you're ready".

Mark and I started to change,

"Are you going with modern under-wear", I asked Mark.

"You're dead right, I am", said Mark. "A Gerbil might jump up and take a nip".

I winced.

"Do Gerbils come from The Holy Land", I said.

"Haven't got a clue", said Mark.

"I wonder what the girls will do about underwear", I said.

"Keep wondering", said Mark.

We finished donning our first century clothing, and stood looking at each other.

"We look like two of the Disciples from my "Boys Book of Bible Stories", I said.

"Well, it's comfortable enough", said Mark.

And it was comfortable. We each had a long linen shirt falling nearly to our ankles, and over that a full length woollen coat, with long sleeves and a hood. A rope sash, with a bag type purse, completed our outfits. We each had sandals for our feet.

"All ready for the school nativity play", said Mark. "I just need a sheep".

"Are you sure about the underwear", I said.

"Oh yes", said Mark. "Definitely sure about the underwear, thank you".

We headed back to the main room. We heard feminine laughter coming from the room opposite ours. The girls were obviously having a lot of fun changing into their new attire.

We found John and Peter in the main room studying their computer screens. They both smiled when they saw us.

"Don't say anything", warned Mark.

Doctor Samuels, Julie, and The Magdalena, joined us a few minutes later. Although they all looked stunning, neither the Doctor, or Julie, could quite manage the natural elegance of The Magdalena, who was completely at home, in what to Her, was normal clothing.

I cast an appraising glance at Miss Parker Smith.

"Modern underwear .... definitely", I thought.

We would perhaps have laughed and joked about our appearance, but the dignified presence of the Magdalena prevented us. She smiled at us, nodding her approval.

Peter gave us each a very expensive "Survival" type watch. They were synchronised to the time on the computer screens.

"We'll activate the cubes on the hour, every hour, said Peter. Whatever you do .... do not enter the cube less than five minutes before or after the hour".

"But will the time there be the same as the time here", I asked.

"Yes it will", said John. "From the beginning of time each hour is followed by the next hour, and the next hour .... and the next hour. An hour took sixty minutes, two thousand years ago .... just as it takes sixty minutes now.

That is a natural law .... and in fact, the science of all this depends upon it. If sixty minutes passes for you, sixty minutes will pass for us here".

"Do we adjust for local time", I asked.

"Definitely not", said Peter. "Keep the watches timed to our computers here. There are no clocks there, in any case".

"When you arrive", said John. "I want Mark to take command. He will obviously work with his specialists, in each of their subjects, as closely as possible .... but Mark will always have the overall safety of the team as his main responsibility".

We stood looking at each other. The originators of the project, Peter and John, in their suits, jackets hanging on the back of their chairs .... the rest of us clothed ready to merge un-noticed, into first century Jerusalem.

"Shall we go", said Mark.

"When you're ready", said Peter, moving towards the nearest computer.

John saw everybody into the "cube". We sorted ourselves out on the levelled sand, and John passed in the various bundles of gear. He made a final check .... and nodded to us.

"Good to go", he said to Peter.

The Magdalena spoke to Julie.

"We are going to have a final prayer", said Julie. "The Magdalena wants us to hold hands in a circle".

We did as requested.

"If you all close your eyes", said Peter, "As soon as The Magdalena finishes Her prayer .... I'll press "send". When you open your eyes .... you'll be there".

"Magdalena .... please begin", said Julie.

It was quite a long prayer. The Magdalena finished. We said "Amen". We opened our eyes .... and we were there.

We were standing on the same level square of sand .... but it had lost four inches of height. Around us the ground rose gently in all directions .... we were in a natural bowl.

It looked just like you would imagine .... yellow brown earth and stones, a few scrubby trees dotted around, one or two patches of dried out grass.

We stepped out of the square, and placed our bundles around the nearest tree. Mark found four steel pegs, and a hammer in his pack. He drove a peg into the ground at each corner of the square of sand, then ran a piece of cord all round, tying it off at one of the corners.

"Right Julie", he said. "You and The Magdalena might as well get going. The sooner we have news the better".

He pulled out a pocket compass, and checked his bearings.

"Road is the other side of that slope", he said." I'll check things are clear first, then call you all up".

He ran to the top of the rise, looked in both directions, then waved for us to join him, on the ridge".

We all went down to the road together.

"Does The Magdalena know where She is", said Mark.

Julie relayed the question.

The Magdalena looked carefully at Her surroundings, and nodded. She spoke to Julie.

"She says we are little more than twenty minutes walk from her home in Bethany", said Julie.

"Off you go then", said Mark.

"Missing you already", said Julie.

Mark went over to the girls.

"Be careful", he said to them. He took The Magdalena's hand, and placed it in Julie's.

"Come back as soon as you can", he said.

We watched them away.

"I would have expected more travellers on the road, in the run up to The Passover", I said.

Mark shrugged.

"Certainly quiet at the moment", he said.

We went back up the slope, and dropped down to our starting place.

"Ok", said Mark, "Lets get that sand built up. We need four inches of extra depth".

We had brought two short handled shovels for this job. The Doctor and I started shovelling.

"No mad rush", said Mark, "We'll do ten minutes each, then stop for a break".

"We should have brought a kettle, so we could make tea", said Doctor Samuels.

"I did", said Mark.

"My hero", said the Doctor.

TWENTY FIVE

"Nigel", said Julie. "Peter tells me you do some writing .... is that true".

"It must be true if Peter says it is", I said. "I think he knows more about me than I do".

"Are you going to write about this", asked Julie.

"I was thinking about that this morning". I said. "Yes .... I think I will .... and the great thing is that nobody will believe a word of it .... apart from us".

"You'd ask Peter and John first though", she said.

"Yes", I said. "I'd have to .... if I was thinking of publishing it".

"It would make a great movie", she said.

"Yes", I said. "I'd thought of that too. Who would you like to play you in the movie".

She pondered.....

"How are things going with Mark", I asked.

She smiled.

"It's good", she said. "Really good. I hope you're not going to tell me off for....".

"No .... I'm not", I said. "That bit at the dinner table when you had to help him with his buttons.......".

Julie blushed.

"I thought you might tell me off because you're religious", she said.

"Me religious ....", I said. "I'm not religious".

"But you believe in .... sorry .... you know there's a God", she said.

"Julie", I said, "I'm not even sure that God is religious".

That stopped her for a moment.

"Nigel", she said. "Can I write a part in your book .... I'd love to have something written by me in a book .... it would be wonderful".

"Julie", I said. "If we survive this .... then yes .... you can write a piece for it".

She nodded.

"Thank you", she said. She paused .... thinking.

"Nigel .... what do you mean about God not being religious".

"That word doesn't mean quite what everybody thinks it means", I said. "Look it up sometime".

"I'll ask Mark", she said.

"Ah .... quite correct", I said. "A girl should always see her husband as the ever flowing fountain of all wisdom and knowledge".

Miss Julie Parker Smith threw a cushion at me.

It missed.

* * *

Julie's narrative.

When The Magdalena and I arrived at her home in Bethany, it was very late afternoon. The sun was falling rapidly into a pinky orange haze on the horizon.

The courtyard was populated by a young tethered goat, chewing on a heap of thistles. The Magdalena ran to it. I knew from my previous visit that the animal was something of a pet in the household. As she petted it .... she called out to her brother and sister. There was no response.

I was beginning to think that the house did seem very quiet ....

The goat resumed it's meal. The Magdalena ruffled it's ears .... and then led me into the house. At the end of a passage that extended the full depth of the building, we turned through the door into the kitchen. An elderly lady, who I knew to be Hannah, the house-keeper, was asleep on a stool, her back resting against the wall.

"Hannah", cried The Magdalena. "Where are Martha and Lazarus".

The old lady woke up. She seemed astonished to see us. There was a very rapid conversation, which I could hardly keep up with. Studying a language from an academic view point is very different to hearing that language used by people who speak it everyday.

The Magdalena turned back to me. I had caught enough of the conversation to understand her expression.

"It's the day of the Passover", she said. "My brother and sister are in the city with our aunt and uncle, to eat the Passover meal tonight".

I looked at Hannah, and The Magdalena, trying to take in what this could mean.

"We have to let the others know this as soon as possible", I said.

The Magdalena hugged Hannah, assured her that she would see her again soon, and despite the house-keepers protests, we ran from the house, and started on the mile long walk back to the team.

We managed, by hurrying, to reach the point where we had joined the road, in little more than twenty minutes.

We went up over the rise, and ran down the slope, to where the others were finishing the job of levelling the earth platform in the cube.

Mark saw us coming. He realised we were hurrying, and I saw him speak to Nigel, and Doctor Samuels, who looked up.

Mark went to his pack, and brought out two plastic bottles of water.

He handed a bottle to each of us. I showed the Magdalena how to manage the cap, and we both drank.

"Catch your breath first", said Mark.

"It's the day of The Passover Feast", I said. "We haven't got two days .... we just have a few hours".

Mark stared at us.

"Are you certain about this", he said.

"Totally certain", I said. "We've been to The Magdalena's house in Bethany, and spoken to the house-keeper. Lazarus, and Martha, are in the city already, for the passover meal tonight".

Mark took a deep breath, and looked at Nigel.

"Alright", he said, "We've had a bit of a surprise .... but in a way, it's good news. It means we can get on with the job straight away .... and that's fine with me. I always hate the "hanging about" part of an operation like this".

Mark cast his eye over the floor they had built in the cube. It stood four inches above the natural base.

"That'll do", he said.

He went into his pack again and brought out something that looked like a tiny mobile phone. He pressed a switch on it's side, and took it to a nearby tree.

"Not much of a tree", he said "But it will have to do".

He reached up and placed the object on a branch, close in against the trunk.

"That's a signal transmitter", he said. "Sends a bleep every three minutes. I've got a receiver that will bring us to that tree even in the pitch dark .... if neccessary".

He came over, and gave me a hug, then kissed me on the forehead. I could tell he was excited to be starting the job.

We gathered up our bundles, sharing the loads between us. The Magdalena indicated that the girls must cover their heads. We tucked our shawls carefully around our faces.

We set off up the slope, but, as before, Mark signalled that we should wait for a moment. Again, he went up to the ridge, looked up and down the road, and then beckoned that we should join him. We ran down to the road .... turned to the right, and set off at a steady pace in the direction of Jerusalem.

We came across one or two other travellers, some resting by the roadside, but they took little notice of us. Some called a greeting.

Whilst Mark and Nigel appeared to be leading, they were in fact, being guided by directions from The Magdalena who walked a pace or two behind them. The Doctor and I brought up the rear.

We were heading for Golgotha .... the Romans preferred place of execution on that side of the city. We knew the tomb we were looking for would be close by.

Just once we attracted some unwanted attention. We passed four Roman soldiers apparently stationed at the roadside to keep an eye on people arriving for The Passover. One of them called out in Latin, causing his fellow guards to laugh. They must have spotted my embarassment. They spoke to each other, and laughed again. It was my fault. I should have left the modern underwear behind.

What is it with men......

*　*　*

And Nigel takes over......

"What were the soldiers laughing about", I said, once we had gone far enough not to be heard.

"Look", said Julie. "Just because I can translate .... doesn't mean I'm always going to".

"But you're wishing you had left a certain item of clothing behind in the twenty first century", I said, laughing.

"How on Earth could you possibly know ....".

I smiled at her.

"Oh", she said. "Of course .... I forgot. Look Nigel , thats just not fair .... stop it".

"Sorry", I said. "Just practising".

"Well stop practising on me", she said.

"Sometimes I can't help it", I said.

We walked on until we could see the walls of Jerusalem on our right hand side. By now, the evening was advancing, and it was very hard to make out much detail in the failing light. The Magdalena told Mark to leave the road, and we found ourselves on a path which was non too level. Mark warned us to tread carefully.

Fifteen minutes later, we arrived at Golgotha. There were four crosses standing there, two with crucifixion victims still in place, but even in the failing light, we could see that they were long dead. It was a thoroughly horrible place. The Magdalena pointed up to a rocky cliff, and we could just make out the jutting rocks, in the rough shape of a skull, that gave the place it's name .... "Golgotha". In Hebrew .... The place of the Skull.

We stood looking round. I hated the place. It was a bare hill top devoid of any vegetation that I could see. It had an atmosphere of despair and desolation, Even the crickets were silent here.

"Seems strange that the walls don't go round this place", said Mark. "From a military point of view, it's not good to have high ground quite so close to the city walls".

By now it was properly dark. All we could see of Jerusalem were a few lights, visible above the walls . The Magdalena stood getting her bearings, then turned away to the left. We went down hill for perhaps ten minutes, and came to an olive plantation. Again she checked her bearings, leading us into the grove, until we came to a wall. It was more of a bank with a ditch beneath it, than a properly built wall. We climbed over the obstruction, into what was obviously a tended garden. Another two minutes brought us to the scene of excavations, and we realised we were looking at a very recently cut tomb.

Mark produced two modern flash lights. He handed one to me, and we stepped forward to examine the entrance. The "door" was a hole in the rock face that even The Magdalena would have to stoop to go through. To the left of this entrance was a large round stone.

"Just like a millstone", I said.

The stone sat on it's edge, in a ditch that ran across the front of the doorway.

Mark and I looked at the way it operated as a door. We rolled the stone to the right until it hit the end of the ditch carved in the rock. The tomb was now closed.

"If that ditch to the left of the stone was back filled", said Mark, "the tomb would be well and truly sealed".

"Simple .... but very effective", I said. "It wouldn't do to be trapped inside".

Mark nodded, and then shone his flashlight inside the tomb. He stooped and went in.

"You can come in", he said, after a moment or two.

We all stooped, one by one, and filed in. It wasn't as big as we had imagined. In fact with all five of us inside, there was no room left.

Doctor Samuels asked me for my flashlight. She examined the four shelves carved in the walls for future interrments.

"There's not much room in here", she said. "It's much smaller than I'd hoped for".

She swung her flashlight around the walls. It was obvious that there was only the one exit.

"It's not big enough to do anything in here", she said. "We can't bring Him in here. We have to get Him back to my surgery as soon as we have Him".

Mark and I looked at each other.

"Time for a re-think", said Mark.

We filed out again. It was a horrible little hole, and I think we were all relieved to be back in the open air.

We stood looking at the tomb.

"It's all going to depend on the time of day .... and how light it is", said Mark. "If we don't get Him down from the cross until its dusk .... then yes .... we might as well head for home. If it's still light .... we'll have to at least bring Him in this direction. To do otherwise would arouse suspicion, in even the simplest person".

"What time were you expecting it to be, when you arrive at the tomb with Jesus", Julie asked.

"That's not a question with a simple answer", I said. "If they carried out the crucifixion between nine and ten in the morning, and if He was on the cross for a maximum of six hours before He died, it would take us to three pm. Then Joseph of Arimathea has to go to Pilate and ask for the body, and Pilate, in turn, has to send for the Centurion to verify that Jesus is dead.

We have no idea of how long it was before Joseph returned here, with permission .... and with Nicodemus".

"Has to be at least two hours", said Mark.

"Two more hours on the cross", said Doctor Samuels. "Not good at all".

"My feeling is", said Mark, that even if we do have to bring Him in this direction .... it won't be for very long".

"I'll do what I can for Him outside", said the doctor, but it mustn't appear that we are attempting treatment. He is meant to be dead".

"I'm going to make tea for us all", said Mark.

He produced a small gas stove, and a kettle, and within six or seven minutes was handing us cups of hot tea.

"No milk", he said. "But there is sugar. I want you all to sugar your tea ....

whether you take sugar or not .... and yes, that is an order, Miss Parker Smith".

He passed out chocolate biscuits. These were another thing that The Magdalena loved . I wondered how girls of her period managed without chocolate.

We sat on the ground, munched our biscuits, and sipped our tea.

"Question", said Mark. "Where are we in the events of the evening, at this moment. Has the Last Supper started yet. Is it over. Julie .... can you ask The Magdalena please".

Julie touched Her gently on the shoulder. She had just started a second chocolate biscuit.

I looked at Her carefully. Her composure was a wonder to me. If I knew somebody close to me was going to suffer .... as Her man was going to suffer ....

Julie asked Her when we could expect Jesus and The Disciples to begin their meal.

"She thinks they will start their Passover meal in about one hour", Julie said.

Mark nodded .... thinking. He turned to Nigel.

"We're getting near to the point where we need your help", he said. "How do you feel about trying".

"Are we going to work from The Magdalena's house at Bethany .... or from here", I asked him.

Mark took a deep breath.

"I've decided to stay here", he said. "It's more secluded than I thought it would be .... and it's close to the action, when the time comes. If the timings in the Gospels are right .:.. we have about fifteen hours until the crucifixion party arrive. I've got enough food and water to see us through".

"But you think that it would be very helpful if we actually knew where we were time-wise", I said.

"It would be very useful", said Mark.

I looked to Doctor Samuels.

"I would like to know His mental state .... particularly His stress level", she said. "Stress is going to be something I have to factor in to any treatment I give".

I looked at them both.

"I can't do it .... not this evening", I said.

The Doctor raised her eyebrows.

"This is the really important night for Jesus", I said. "He has to decide whether He will stay in the Garden of Gethsemane, and wait for the arrest .... or whether He will escape. It's that waiting .... when He knows what is in store for Him .... that sets Him apart from all other men. The future rests on His decision tonight. Only He can make that decision".

"I never saw it quite like that before", said Mark. "He could have escaped .... but He chose not to. He chose to stay".

"Yes", I said, "And you can feel His relief in the Gospel accounts .... when the arresting party arrive .... and the responsibility of the decision is lifted from Him. It's too late to make choices. He has passed the final test".

There was a long silence. The crickets did what crickets do ....

The Magdalena took Julie's hand. She stood, and pulled her up, speaking softly as she rose.

"The Magdalena thinks She must join The Disciples now .... and She wants me to be with Her", Julie said.

"Are you actually going to be there .... at The Last Supper." I said, rising myself.

"I don't know", she said. "I thought I would be staying here .... but it seems not".

"To be there .... at that supper .... would be amazing", I said.

The Magdalena released Julie, and came to where I was standing. She embraced me .... and we stayed in each others arms, eyes closed, for a minute or more.

"The Magdalena has asked that I say a prayer", I said. "It's my turn....".

We all joined hands. The Magdalena had us well trained by this time.

"Awesome God", I said. "If this mission is of your will .... then let your purpose be fulfilled. Watch over us, and give us strength, and courage, conviction, and inspiration, in the hours ahead. Amen".

And the team said Amen.

And The Magdalena took Julie's hand and led her away into the garden.

TWENTY SIX

We watched The Magdalena and Julie disappear amongst the olive trees. The evening had cooled a little .... it was early Spring here .... and Mark suggested we light a fire.

"Aren't we going to draw attention to ourselves", I asked.

"I don't think it's likely", he said. "Just about everybody is in the City. Nobody is going to be coming out to visit a tomb at this time of the day".

We started to gather some wood .... there was plenty to be had .... and Mark started building the fire.

He was about to light it, when he stiffened, listening ....

I had heard it too .... a cough .... from the path that Julie and The Magdalena had taken. We slipped back amongst the trees.

Two men came up to the tomb. They were carrying a large bundle, neatly wrapped, and tied, on two wooden poles .... as a stretcher would be carried.

They stopped at the entrance, put their burden on the ground, and undid the cords that bound it all together.

One of them knelt on the ground, placed something on a stone in front of him .... and started to blow. A flame appeared. I realised they had brought a live coal, and a tinder box, with them. They lit a small oil lamp, and carrying the bundle .... one at each end .... they disappeared into the tomb.

We stayed still .... watching.

"It's amazing they haven't seen our bundles of gear", I whispered to Mark.

"Concentrating on what they're doing", said Mark.

We continued to wait.

After five minutes or so, the men reappeared. One of them gathered up the two poles, and pushed them into some bushes to the side of the tomb.

And then they astonished us.

They held the lamp up so their faces were visible, and one of them called:

"Mark, Nigel, Doctor".

We were really not expecting this. His pronunciation was far from perfect, but the intention was plain enough. They knew we were there …. and we were being called to show ourselves.

"It's Ok", said Mark. "The Magdalena must have told them we are here …. we can step out and meet them".

"But we haven't got Julie to interpret for us", I said.

"I'll try some latin", said Mark. "Might be good enough for a few words".

We stepped out of the trees. Our visitors came forward to greet us.

To my surprise both men seemed to understand Mark's latin. They were both in their thirties, fairly well dressed, and you would have to say that they were of a serious disposition …. a very serious disposition indeed.

Mark talked to them for a few minutes …. then turned to me.

"They are servants of Joseph of Arimathea", he said."This is his garden.They met Julie and The Magdalena at the entrance. They were coming to deliver the bundle to the tomb".

"Alhoes and Mhyrr perhaps", said the Doctor.

The two men seemed anxious to be away. Hanging around a tomb, when there was celebration at home …. I could understand them. Before they left, however, they came to the Doctor and I, and held our hands briefly, and spoke to us.

"They wish us God's blessing for tomorrow", said Mark.

We all said our thanks to them. Mark translated into latin …. and they returned to the path through the garden.

Mark lit his fire, using a modern cigarette lighter, built up a wigwam shape using twigs, and got out his tea equipment again.

"Time for our own "Passover Feast", he said.

Simon had put together a picnic not dissimilar to the one we had eaten for lunch a few days ago. Mark spread it all out on a blanket, and made the tea. For fifteen minutes or so we ate in relative silence. We were all thinking about the next twenty four hours.

"Are there any plans for tomorrow", I asked Mark.

"I'm reluctant to make too many plans, when all I have is a two thousand year old account of events to base them on", said Mark. " We might go up to the crucifixion site in the morning, and get the lay of the land. I'll put my uniform on. It's the uniform of a Centurion .... so I can pull rank on just about anybody we might encounter. I'm also hoping that I might be able to use my rank to send away the guard, after the crucifixion .... and possibly shorten the amount of time Jesus has to spend nailed to the cross".

"Even minutes less would help", said the Doctor.

"The other unknown", said Mark, "is how many people are likely to be there. Are we talking a cast of thousands .... or in reality .... will it just be a relatively small group of the sort of people who like to watch cruelty. I don't know".

"Did you know", I said, "that the last execution in Britain by "Hanging, drawing, and quartering", was carried out in public, on Southsea common near Portsmouth, in 1782. Ten thousand people turned up to watch".

".... and enjoyed every moment of it, no doubt", said Doctor Samuels. "Thank God that we've all moved on a bit since then".

"I think it should be Jesus we thank for that", I said.

She nodded thoughtfully.

"I hope to be able to do just that", she said.

"In a way", said Mark, "a large crowd will make it easier for us to do what we want amongst the chaos .... but my feeling is that we shouldn't expect too many people. I think Pilate wanted the whole thing wrapped up before the population realised what was happening .... hence the early start.

The wine will have been flowing at the feasting, and not too many people will be keen to get up early, and trudge up to Golgotha .... even if they have heard about the sentencing of Jesus. I think we'll see a hundred at the very most .... and they're likely to drift away once the worse of the screaming has stopped".

I winced.

"Yes", said Mark. "I'm afraid we are going to hear a lot of screaming tomorrow .... and not much we can do about it. There will be at least three people being crucified .... and it's not a pretty site .... as the Doctor explained to us".

We lapsed into silence. There were plenty of crickets here, even if it was early in the year.

It was Doctor Samuels who brought us back to the task in hand. She went to her own bundle of equiment, and came back with an earthenware jar sealed by a large cork. She handed it to me.

"You have a job tomorrow Nigel", she said. "The Gospels describe Jesus drinking from a sponge dipped in vinegar, just before "He gave up his spirit". Whilst I'm reasonably sure of what might have been on that sponge .... it will be easier for me if the sponge is dipped in this jar. One mouthful of this .... and He'll go out like a light .... and I will know exactly what I'm dealing with when I come to revive Him".

"What's in it", I asked her.

She told me. It was fairly un-pronouncable, and definitely un-spellable.

"Ok .... If I can do it ..... I will", I said.

There was a call from the direction of the path .... it was Julie .... with one of our visitors from earlier .... the younger of the two .... with a blanket under his arm.

Mark jumped up and embraced Julie.

"We weren't expecting you until tomorrow", he said.

"I know", said Julie. "We went to Joseph of Arimathea's house first. The Magdalena told him you were here by the tomb. He had sent Nicodemus and Phillip up here with a bundle of herbs. We met them at the lower entrance to the garden. Joseph gave us some supper, and while we were eating .... word came for The Magdalena that Jesus wanted to see her. When Nicodemus and Phillip returned, Joseph suggested that I be brought back here. He didn't think it was safe for me to stay in the City".

Mark nodded.

"I'm glad to have you back", he said. "Is Phillip staying with us".

"He'll stay until dawn", said Julie.

Mark waved Phillip to a place by the fire, and spoke a few words to him in latin. Phillip replied .... smiled at each of us in turn .... then wrapped his blanket around him, and lay down, with his feet to the fire.

"He begs our indulgence", said Mark. "He has had a very long day, and he must sleep for a while".

"I couldn't sleep if I tried", said Julie.

"Nor me", I said.

" You amateurs", said Mark, smiling. "Well I can sleep .... and it would be best if I sleep now. You two can wake me when you're ready to turn in. Somebody should stay awake .... and you two will find that difficult after two in the morning. I know what happens. You'll have real trouble keeping your eyelids open. I'll take over when you're ready for bed".

With that .... he rolled himself into a blanket next to Phillip .... and appeared to fall asleep instantly.

"I'm going to sleep now as well", said Doctor Samuels. She had brought a light sleeping bag.

We left her tucking herself in. ·

We settled under a tree a dozen or so yards away. We could talk there without disturbing the others.

In an old black and white movie, I would have produced a cigarette case at this point. Julie would accept a cigarette from me, and we would light up. There would be a pause, as we began to smoke. We would exhale long and slowly before speaking ....

"Nigel", said Julie, eventually. "What do you think is going to happen tomorrow".

I took my imaginary cigarette from my mouth, pausing to think ....

"To some extent, we are going to have to be ready for surprises", I said. "As Mark said .... we are relying on two thousand year old accounts of what happened".

"I did actually read The New Testament", said Julie. "It's so strange how it goes into immense detail over some incidents .... the Disciples catching one hundred and fifty three fish .... for example .... while there is next to no detail on some really important things like the crucifixion".

"That's one of the quirky things about The Holy Bible", I said. "But having said that .... the modern Bible historians tell us that it can, and should, be relied on as an account of the life of Jesus. It fulfils their criteria as historical evidence".

"We're going to be able to tell them how accurate their evidence is, by the end of tomorrow", said Julie.

"We're going to see how accurate it is", I said. "I'm not sure that we'll be able to tell anybody about it".

There was a pause. Julie would have blown smoke rings into the mediterranean air .... had she been smoking.

"The Magdalena told me about going to Church with you", she said. "She thought it was wonderful .... everybody She met was so friendly.

I laughed.

"I would have loved to tell them who She really was", I said.

"Why didn't you", said Julie.

I laughed again.

"Would you have believed it", I said.

"I guess not", she said.

We smoked on .... or at least .... we would have done .... if this was an old black and white movie.

"Nigel", said Julie.

"Yes Julie", I said.

"The Magdalena told me that She heard you praying in a different language".

I laughed.

"Yes", I said. "She would have heard me praying "in tongues".

"You actually pray in tongues", said Julie, turning towards me.

"I do", I said.

"Tell me about it", she said. "I'm interested in anything to do with languages".

I paused .... taking a long pull on my cigarette.

"Right", I said. "I took The Magdalena to The Destiny Centre .... an African based Pentecostal Church".

"How did you start to go there", said Julie.

I laughed.

"Awesome God organised that surprise", I said.

"Nigel", said Julie. "Why do you say "Awesome God".

I smiled thoughtfully.

"I picked up the phrase from a very lovely young lady who used to work for me at events", I said, "She always began her prayers with "Awesome God".

Julie produced her own virtual cigarette case. I took one when offered. She produced a virtual lighter ....

"You were starting to tell me about praying in tongues", she said.

"Yes", I said. "Some people get quite wound up about the issue of praying "in tongues".... usually because they haven't seen it used .... and don't understand how it is used".

"Tell me". said Julie.

"Ok", I said. "Tongues" is a prayer language .... usually just a few phrases .... given to you by The Holy Spirit.

You might receive the gift at any age, and under any circumstances .... and those who have been given it, will always have a story of how they received it. In my case .... it's very simple. The leading Pastors in the Church anounced during a service that they were going to pray directly to The Holy Spirit. They would pray that those who didn't yet have their "prayer language", might receive it that evening. Those who were interested were asked to step up to the altar. I went forward .... and that evening, I was given the phrases I still use now".

"Can I hear them", asked Julie.

I thought for a moment.

"I'd have to explain how I use the gift, before I do that", I said.

"But why can't you just pray in English", said Julie.

"It's much easier in "tongues", I said. "You can pray for much longer".

"In the Churches I've been to", said Julie, "the prayers only last a minute or two".

"Yes", I said, "But in my church, there are prayer sessions that last up to two and a half hours .... and to pray for that length of time .... it would be really really difficult without "tongues".

"Two and a half hours ....", said Julie.

"Yes", I said. "That would be a special session .... but the normal Friday night session lasts for ninety minutes .... and that is ninety minutes spent simply praying .... nothing else".

"I don't see how you can do that", said Julie. "Ninety minutes simply praying....".

"But if you use "tongues", I said, "that ninety minutes goes by very quickly .... it's almost like time itself is altered".

"But does each person have a different prayer language", Julie asked.

"Yes", I said. "Everybody who has "The gift of tongues" uses phrases that are unique to them .... the phrases that they were given".

"But how do you understand each other", she said.

I sighed.

"You don't need to understand each other", I said. "You are talking directly to God. He gave you the phrases you have .... so He understands what you are saying".

"So how does a prayer session work at your Church", said Julie.

"Ok", I said, "Lets say that you have thirty people turn up for a Friday night prayer session. One of the Pastors will go onto the stage, and will introduce the topic that you are going to pray about. He .... or she .... will start the prayers using ordinary English .... and invite everybody to lift up their voices in prayer .... to join in. Most people do start to pray in English .... but after a few minutes .... they naturally start to use their prayer language phrases. They are then praying "in tongues". A prayer on one topic can last up to fifteen minutes .... but you can continue indefinitely if you use your prayer language".

Julie nodded thoughtfully.

"I'd love to see this in operation", she said.

"No problem", I said. "Come with me to a service, and you can take part".

"I think I would feel very awkward", she said.

I laughed.

"No need to", I said. "You'll soon get the hang of it".

"But I haven't got the gift of tongues", she said.

"Well if you like, we could pray that you be given it", I said.

"Can we do that .... would it work with just the two of us", she said.

"That", I said, "is the decision of The Holy Spirit. We can ask .... but it's The Holy Spirit who gives you the gift".

"Could we pray for me to be given the gift now .... right here", said Julie.

I shook my head.

"Not possible", I said. "You are asking for a gift from The Holy Spirit .... and The Holy Spirit only comes to the world of men, when Jesus has died .... and returned to His Father. Jesus tells the Disciples that He must leave them .... so that The Spirit can come".

"And Jesus is till here at the moment ....", she said.

I nodded. I finished that second cigarette.

"You'll have to wait", I said.

"But if we do rescue Him ....", she said.

"Yes", I said. " If we do rescue Him ....".

There was a long silence. We finished our cigarettes, and buried the stubs neatly in the dry ground.

"I'm for bed", said Julie. "I'll wake Mark".

I laughed.

Julie looked puzzled .... and then blushed.

"That came out wrong didn't it", she said.

"Heard of Freud", I asked.

Julie looked round for something to throw at me.

"Julie", I said.

"What now", she said.

"Might be better if you don't "stand out" in the crowd so much tomorrow", I said.

She looked at me and laughed.

"Ok", she said, "I'll sort it".

"Are you going to wake Mark now", I said.

"No .... I'm not", she said. "You can do it".

"I'll tell him you were too shy", I said.

"Like he's going to believe that ....", she said.

"You go to bed", I said. "I'm going to sit here a while".

"Will you be Ok without somebody to talk to", she said.

"Julie", I said, "I've always got Somebody to talk to".

She kissed me on the cheek.

"Good night", she said. "Don't forget to wake Mark".

She walked back to the fire.

I sat listening to the crickets. I lit a third cigarette.

This virtual smoking would have to stop. There could be health issues.

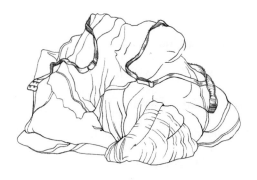

"Well if we are …. we're definitely not going together", said Mark.

"I'm just fine as I am", I said …. hastily.

"That's it", said Mark. "Nigel's a recovery man. I'm a soldier. We don't do morning washes".

"But you'd both feel so much fresher", said Doctor Samuels …. with that familiar twinkle in her eyes.

"I think Mark is ….".

"Nigel ….", warned Mark.

"Sorry", I said.

"Breakfast", said Mark.

Simon had packed us a mediterranean style breakfast of bread, cheeses, olives …. and small pots of yoghurt.

"Do real men eat yoghurt", I asked, as Mark passed me my pot.

"Yoghurt is really good for your sperm count", said Doctor Samuels.

"Is that really a medical fact", asked Mark.

"Has to be true", she said. "Just look at it".

We sighed …. and ate our yoghurts.

*　*　*

The air began to warm. There was every sign that we were in for a fine warm spring day.

"Lovely day for a crucifixion", Mark said.

"Julie", said Doctor Samuels. "I'd like to run through with you some of the things you can do to help me later today. How are you with naked men covered in blood …. lots of blood".

Julie looked uncertain.

"Julie", Mark said. "The secret is to shut off your emotions completely. Just do what has to be done .... and know that by doing that .... you're being part of the team. That's the best way to help everybody".

"I'd agree with that", I said.

"But you won't be able to do that yourself", said Julie.

"No", I said. "I have to do just the opposite .... that's why I'm here".

"Let's leave them to talk through their first aid plans", said Mark. "And while they're doing that .... I'd like to check through my uniform and weapons. Perhaps have a dress rehearsal .... if you can give me a hand".

We undid the relevant bundles, and layed out Marks uniform. He assembled the pilum .... the spear.

"With help", said Mark, "I can get ready for action in about eight minutes. I still haven't decided the best moment to become the Roman soldier. I'm sort of planning to watch the crucifixions as a civilian .... wait for things to settle down a bit .... then come back here to change .... but I'll need you to help me".

We spent the next twenty minutes, or so, practising getting Mark into his uniform. Once we'd worked out the best order .... we could do it in little more than five minutes. Mark seemed happy enough with that timing.

He changed back to his ordinary clothes, and we packed up his Roman gear again .... but trying to keep it in some sort of logical order.

"Where are we going to leave it, so it will be safe", I said.

"Not a problem", said Mark. "Phillip is going to watch things here. He doesn't want to see the crucifixions. He's seen too many".

Mark went off to make more tea .... and I decided .... just to fill in time really .... to have a second look inside the tomb. I collected a flashlight .... and called over to Mark.

I pointed at the tomb door. Mark nodded.

Inside .... I was again surprised by how small it was. Perhaps just room enough for four people to lay side by side on the floor. The ceiling was low .... just clear of the top of my head. There were four shelves, about twenty inches deep, carved into the walls. One of them contained the bundle that Joseph's men had brought last night. I bent .... and sniffed at it. There was a strong aroma of herbs.

There was no form of decoration on the tomb walls .... nothing to see of note. I scanned the flashlight beam around the walls one last time, and started to leave. But something had caught the corner of my eye.

On the floor .... barely discernible .... there appeared to be a rectangular mark, about seven feet long, and three feet wide. It wasn't so much marked on the floor .... more that this rectangular shape seemed to be a different colour to the rest of the tomb. It's outline had been much scuffed out by the passage of feet. If I looked directly at the outline .... I couldn't see anything. But if I looked indirectly at the area .... so I was using the more light sensitive part of my eyes .... the rectangle was just about visible.

I was just about to call out to Mark, to ask him to come and look at what I'd found .... when I heard voices outside the tomb .... and Mark called me.

Outside, I found Mark, and Julie, in conversation with Phillip. Julie took over the dialogue .... using Aramaic. Mark listened a few moments longer, then called to me.

"We're off", he said. "The crucifixion party are outside the city walls .... on their way here".

I gave a final glance at the tomb .... and unable to resist a souvenir .... I stooped and picked up a fresh rock chipping. A Genuine Rock Fragment from the Original Tomb of Jesus of Nazareth.

Then I had a very unpleasant thought. Later that day .... If I had the mind to .... I'd be able to add A Fragment of the One True Cross, to my collection of Sacred Relics. I threw the rock chipping back to where it had come from.

Mark was mustering his troops. He asked for our wrist watches, took the straps off, and attached a cord to each one, so we could hang them around our necks. He made a final inspection, then asked Julie to confirm that Phillip was going to stay, and guard our gear.

With everything organised, he told Julie to take the lead, and we set off down the path that went through the garden. As we walked, Mark explained that the plan was to tag along on the end of the execution party, as they came past the lower gate. He felt it would look more natural than joining further up .... at the top of the garden.

There was no real reason to be worried about making our appearance in public .... as it were. Our clothing fitted in well enough, as we knew from our previous walk along the road from Bethany. And if our faces and skin tones were a little noticeable .... well there were plenty of strangers "in town" for The Passover.

But I was nervous .... very nervous. I didn't even feel under enormous pressure to fullfil my role. I was sure that the others could manage without me .... if neccessary.

My nervousness came, I knew well enough, from the tension. A tension caused by knowing that step by tiny step, we were drawing closer, and closer, to the execution. I had never been able to watch even a movie which has the build up to an execution, as part of the story. I would get more and more tense, as the preparations continued .... until I would have to switch off the television .... or leave the cinema. If I stayed .... I would become physically sick.

And here I was on my way to a real execution .... by the most barbaric, and inhumane method ever devised. And the victim .... the most famous man who ever lived on Earth. Jesus of Nazareth.

I came up beside the Doctor.

"I'm getting very tense .... almost distressed". I said.

She nodded, glanced at me, and reached into her robe.

"I thought you might begin to feel like that", she said. "I want you to chew this".

She put a squarish yellow tablet in my hand.

"It's like a chewy sweet with a sugar coating", she said. "Just chew it slowly, and it'll help with the tension".

I did as instructed. Just the act of chewing helped.

"Banana flavour", I said.

"That's it ", she said. "Be a good patient now .... and keep chewing for me".

TWENTY EIGHT

The Langdon Chase Hotel sits on the hill-side above lake Windermere. It has to be one of the loveliest hotels in Britain. Dating from the eighteen ninetys, it was originally built as a private country house. A wealthy northern industrialist intended it as a present for his young Italian wife.

The Hotel grounds run down to the water's edge .... many of the rooms have lake views .... and it is perhaps the calming influence created by the famous stretch of water that gives the hotel it's uniquely peaceful atmosphere.

It is in every detail the most perfect example of an English country house hotel. If you want to escape for a few days, if you want to sit and reflect, if you want to be looked after, to be pampered, in superbly comfortable surroundings .... the Langdon Chase Hotel cannot be beaten.

It is an expensive hotel .... yes .... but it is not ridiculously expensive .... and it has remained a very popular retreat from the modern world since it became a hotel in the nineteen thirties.

Jonathan Cape had studied the Hotel's brochure, in great detail, before driving up from London. It would have been lovely to have booked a room .... but, on reflection, he had decided to wait until his partner Deborah could join him. It would be a treat that she would enjoy very much indeed.

He must remember to check that the towels were suitably soft and fluffy. Just how do hotels do that ....

It hadn't been a bad trip up the motorway. He hadn't got away quite as early as he hoped .... but by substituting sandwiches and crisps, in the car, for a proper lunch stop, he managed to arrive comfortably on time for his appointment at three thirty.

The driveway to the hotel proper was beautifully tended. Brushed golden shingle .... two car width .... and absolutely no speed humps. A discreet sign every two hundred metres reminded guests to drive sedately.

His boss had loaned him the company deluxe transport .... a fully dressed

4x4. The gravel drive crunched appropriately beneath it's tyres, as he arrived at the Hotel's frontage. He slowed to a crawl, spotted a parking space, and berthed the car between a Rolls Royce, and a Mercedes. A vintage Mercedes.

He climbed out, and stretched. It had been a long drive. The hotel was catching the last of the sun on this February afternoon. It would be distinctly chilly in an hour or so .... and once again .... he wished he had booked in for the night.

He collected his briefcase from the rear seat, locked up, and headed for the main entrance.

At the top of the steps, a uniformed commissionaire waited patiently.

"Good afternoon", he said. "Have I the pleasure of welcoming Mr Jonathan Cape".

Jonathan was a little taken aback.

"You do indeed", he said. "Mr Jonathan Cape to see Mr Nigel White. I have an appointment for three thirty".

"Yes Mr Cape", said the commissionaire. "Mr White asked me to greet you personally. I know he is looking forward to your meeting".

He pushed open the oak framed doors .

"I'll take you as far as reception", he said.

There were two very smartly dressed young women on the reception desk. Black skirts, dazzlingly white blouses, hair tied back in pony tails.

"Ah Sarah", said the commissionaire. "This is Mr Jonathan Cape. He has an appointment with Mr White at three thirty".

Sarah smiled. She checked her wrist watch.

"Thank you John", she said. "I'll take Mr Cape through to the sun lounge".

The commissionaire wished Jonathan a pleasant afternoon, and returned to his post.

"If you'd like to follow me ....", said Sarah.

Jonathan nodded.

"Are you staying with us tonight", said the receptionist.

She walked very crisply .... and at quite a pace.

"Sadly no", said Jonathan, "I really do have to be back in London for tomorrow morning. But I hope to book a stay with you in the near future. I want to bring my partner here for a short break".

"We shall look forward to that", said Sarah.

She held open the third set of doors.

"This is our sun lounge", she said. "It's a very popular room because it looks out over the lake. It catches the afternoon sun .... and we serve afternoon tea here at three forty five, every day .... so you are just in time".

It was a largish room .... very much an Edwardian conservatory .... but furnished with comfortable arm chairs, around low tables. The view across the water made the room very special. It was not difficult to understand it's popularity.

"We'll find Mr White by the fire", Sarah said.

She led the way across the room to the far right wall. There was a fireplace there .... a log fire burning well .... baskets of split logs to either side.

One arm chair was positioned to take advantage of the fire .... but also to retain a view of the lake.

Jonathan stayed respectfully a yard or so behind, as Sarah approached the chair. She reached down, and touched it's occupant gently on the hand.

"Mr White .... it's Mr Cape to see you", she said.

The chair's occupant rose.

"Thank you Sarah", he said.

He stood and turned to greet his visitor.

Sarah stepped back.

"Shall I tell Polly "tea for two", she said.

"Absolutely Sarah", the man said. "And Danish pastries for both of us please".

Sarah smiled.

"Polly will be with you in five minutes", she said.

"Thank you Sarah", said the man.

This short exchange had given Jonathan a moment to study the man he had travelled from London to see.

And he was puzzled. Very puzzled.

He had expected somebody much older. In fact, by his reckoning, some twenty years older. The man in front of him could barely be described as being in his early sixties .... but ....

"Mr Cape .... it's a pleasure to see you .... did your trip go smoothly".

Jonathan stepped forward, and the two men shook hands.

"Yes, I had a good trip", he said. "Not too much traffic at this time of the year".

"But aren't we lucky with the sun ....".

The man waved towards the conservatory windows. The lake was now in the shadow of the surrounding hills, but the tops of the trees, in the Hotel grounds,were still catching the winter sunlight.

He motioned Jonathan to the opposite arm chair. Jonathan sat down. He was uncertain. He had to clarify things. He reached down for his briefcase, placed it squarely on his lap, opened it, and removed a book. He placed the book, title upwards, on the table.

"Mr White", he said. "I just need to be quite sure of things. Are you the Mr Nigel White who wrote this book".

Mr White .... if indeed it was Mr White .... leaned forwards, and picked up the book. He opened it, produced a large magnifying glass from his pocket, and studied the frontispiece.

"This is a first edition", he said. "And what's even more remarkable .... it isn't signed by the author. There weren't many of the first edition that I didn't sign. This one escaped".

"Then you are ....".

"Yes", said Nigel White smiling . "I am the very same Nigel White who wrote "get Him out". The very same .... I promise you".

Johnathan paused.

"I do apologise", he said. "It's just that ....".

Nigel laughed.

"Let me guess", he said. "You expected me to be older".

"Well Yes .... I must admit I was expecting somebody rather older", he said.

"It must be the wonderful air here at The Langdon Chase", said Nigel. "It's well known to be very invigorating .... and of course .... the food is quite wonderful".

Jonathan looked a little doubtful.

Afternoon tea arrived.

"I've brought a small plate of sandwiches, as well as the pastries", said the waitress, whose name badge confirmed that she was the promised "Polly".

"Sarah thought your guest might be be hungry".

"Well Polly, even if he's not, I shall do them justice", said Nigel. "Thank Sarah for the thought".

"Would you pour the tea please Mr Cape", said Nigel. "Not too much milk .... no sugar".

Jonathan obliged .... and passed the cup and saucer.

"It's Jonathan", he said. "I am sorry for questioning you in that way. Its just that ....".

"Jonathan, its not a problem", said Nigel. "It's not the first time it has happened .... and by God's grace .... I hope it won't be the last".

They took a sandwich each. Jonathan reflected on the "garage sandwich" he'd eaten for lunch. To be fair to it .... it had been a perfectly nice sandwich .... but it definitely hadn't been a "Langdon Chase Afternoon Tea in the Conservatory" sandwich. Again he wished he'd booked in.

Nigel sipped his tea.

"Now Jonathan", he said. "What has brought you all the way from London, on a chilly winter afternoon, to see an author who only ever wrote one book .... and that twenty something years ago".

Jonathan smiled thoughtfully.

"I'm representing Gilson and Howes, Publishers", he said. "You may have heard that we recently bought Fellows & Sons, who published your book. As such, we have acquired the publishing rights to "get Him out".

Nigel nodded.

"I do know about this", he said. "My agent keeps me informed of developements. I don't think you've driven all this way to tell me about that".

"No, it's true .... I haven't", said Jonathan. "I want to talk to you about the book. It's coming up to the twenty first anniversary of the original publication .... and we are interested in producing what you might call a "Special Edition".

"With a new dust jacket, a presentation box, a new forward by the author, and colour illustrations by a current artist. That sort of thing", Nigel asked.

"No", said Jonathan, "not that sort of thing at all".

"Then what ....".

"We'd like to publish the first edition", said Jonathan.

Nigel looked closely at his visitor.

Jonathan sat quietly .... waiting for the response.

Nigel seemed to choose his words carefully.

"But you have the first edition there on the table", he said.

"Do I .... really", said Jonathan.

He sat back .... cradling his tea cup .... watching the author carefully.

Nigel leaned forwards, took a Danish pastry, placed it on his tea plate, and cut it carefully into four.

"What makes you think that's not the first edition", he said.

Jonathan took a deep breath.

"I read your book for the first time when I was about twelve years old", he said. "Our R.E. teacher at school said I would find it interesting. I did find it very interesting .... as did a number of my friends. It took a subject that might look boring .... and turned it on it's head. I read it over and over again".

"I'm very pleased that it made such an impression", said Nigel.

"One of the fascinating things about the book .... is trying to work out how much of it is fact .... and how much of it is fiction", said Jonathan.

Nigel laughed.

"I designed it like that", he said.

"I think that becomes obvious after several reads", said Jonathan. "But there is another interesting thing that begins to emerge, as you get to know the book really well".

"And what's that", said Nigel. He started on the third quarter of his pastry. He kept his eyes firmly on his visitor's face.

Jonathan smiled.

"The book changes after chapter twenty seven", he said. "In fact, I don't believe you wrote the subsequent chapters".

He reached forward for another sandwich. Sarah had been right. That garage lunch seemed ancient history.

"Why", said Nigel.

Jonathan reached for his tea. The cup was empty. He poured himself a second cup.

"Ok", he said. "After the end of chapter twenty seven, the writing style is a little different. It's very similar .... but there is a difference.

Then there are the personal details that you put in. Very personal in some instances .... particularly in the earlier chapters .... they simply stop.

But most noticeable of all .... the references to books and films and TV .... and it's obvious that you really enjoyed putting them in. Again .... they simply stop happening after chapter twenty seven. There are non at all".

"And what do you deduce from all these observations", asked Nigel.

"Somebody else .... and I suspect Miss Parker Smith ....".

"You mean Mrs Mark Rossi", said Nigel.

"They did marry then", said Jonathan.

"They did indeed", said Nigel. "One of the most fun weddings I've ever been to".

"So was it "Julie", who wrote chapter twenty eight onwards", Jonathan asked.

Nigel looked thoughtfully at his empty plate. A second Danish pastry was always tempting .... but it did tend to spoil supper.

"Suppose Julie Parker Smith did finish the book", Nigel said. "Why do you think that might have happened".

Jonathan looked a little nervously accross the table. He took a deep breath.

"Because", he said, "I think the book is true fact .... true fact in extraordinary detail .... until the end of chapter twenty seven. After that .... I suspect that the final chapters are pure fiction.

I believe that what actually happened that day .... the day of the crucifixion .... is written in the real first edition. A first edition which you decided you could not publish.

And because you couldn't bring yourself to write a fictional ending .... Julie stepped in".

There was a long pause. Nigel lowered his eyes. Jonathan thought he had closed them. The silence continued. Jonathan noticed that his companions lips were moving.

He waited.

Polly brought fresh tea.

Nigel looked up at her.

"Polly", he said, "Would you be so kind as to bring an extra cup please".

The waitress looked at him a little uncertainly.

Nigel nodded.

"Yes .... if you could please, Polly", he said.

Polly left

Nigel leaned forward to pour the tea .... and as his jacket slid up a little, revealing his shirt sleeves .... Jonathan noticed the tightly fitting cuffs, each with their silver cuff links, fashioned after the cross.

"Nigel", asked Jonathan. "Do you still wear that same cross around your neck .... the one in the book".

Nigel nodded.

"Yes .... I still wear it", he said.

"May I see it", said Jonathan.

Nigel smiled.

"Jonathan", he said. "I will show you greater wonders than these".

He lapsed into silence.

Polly returned with a third cup, plate, and saucer.

"Just a few minutes Nigel", she said.

He nodded.

Jonathan looked at the cake on the third plate. There appeared to be frost .... real frost on the sponge.

Nigel rose from his arm chair. Polly had returned. From the corner of his eye, Jonathan saw that she had somebody with her.

Jonathan stood to greet the new guest. As he turned, Polly stepped aside.

Standing in front of Jonathan was a girl .... perhaps seventeen or eighteen years old. She had dark hair, and dark lashes, and olive tinted skin. She held out her hands in greeting. She spoke.

Jonathan did not recognise the language. He looked to Nigel.

"That's first century Aramaic", said Nigel.

Jonathan took her hands. The girl smiled.

"Jonathan, this is Mary of Magdala .... Mary Magdalene", Nigel said.

The Magdalena took Jonathan in her arms. She had discovered that it stopped people collapsing onto their knees.

She had found this reaction to her presence a remarkably trying part of her visits to this time and place.

She was really, at heart, a quiet village girl. It was her boyfriend who was famous.

The Magdalena released Jonathan. She beckoned him to be seated. Polly had brought a third chair. The Magdalena sat.

"Mr Cape", she said. "Do you know Jesus".

Jonathan stared at her. He seemed to have lost his voice.

Nigel smiled. He remembered his first meeting with this young girl.

Jonathan would regain his composure in a minute or two.

Nigel poured a third cup .... and passed it to Mary of Magdala.

The Magdalena smiled at him. She also remembered.

TWENTY NINE

The Magdalena sat quietly, and ate her slice of baked alaska. That curious combination of heat and chill still fascinated her. She watched Nigel persuading Jonathan to stay the night. She drank her tea. She thought about her baby daughter, Madeleine.

Upstairs, Samantha, the Nanny, was putting little Madeleine to bed.

Jonathan's stay had become a certainty when Sarah, the receptionist, had come to tell him that an unexpected snow fall was imminent .... and if he did intend to return to London that night .... it would be the advice of the Langdon Chase .... based on past experience .... that he leave whilst the roads were still clear. Snow fall here could be very sudden .... and very heavy.

Jonathan decided to stay.

The Magdalena reflected that her life would have been very different if She had taken her Father's advice, and married that nice young tax collector, Jabel, from her home village of Magdala. She had almost decided to .... but then Jesus had come back.

He'd been away for seventeen years. But it had really only ever been Jesus. She knew that the moment she saw Him again.

Her Father had despaired.

"He'll come to no good", he had warned her.

Now that really was a matter of opinion, The Magdalena reflected.

She gathered some English words together, explained that She must return to her daughter, and told Jonathan that She hoped to see him at dinner.

The two men rose .... and The Magdalena left the room. As always, every eye turned to watch Her depart.

Jonathan turned back towards Nigel.

"I think I'd better phone my boss", he said. "....and my partner Deborah".

"If you go back to reception, Sarah will sort you out with a room", Nigel said.

Jonathan headed for the door .... then he turned back.

"Nigel", he said. "The Magdalena is the same age as she was in your book".

"That's true", Nigel said.

"But that was twenty years ago".

"Not for the Magdalena", Nigel said, "because she is visiting us just one year after her first visit here".

Jonathan shook his head in confusion.

"Perfectly simple", said Nigel. "Her age here depends on the point during Her life that we lift Her from".

"I'll go and book in", said Jonathan.

Nigel watched him go. He beckoned to Polly.

"Polly, could you fetch my stick please .... and just walk me to the lift. I'd better sort some evening clothes out for our guest".

Polly brought a walking stick from the stand in the corner of the sun lounge.

Nigel stood up .... very straight. Polly took his arm .... and they progressed slowly to the lift in the passageway. Slowly is perhaps not quite the right word. Nigel walked carefully .... as though he must check every footfall for security before trusting to it. Like a man walking on thin ice.

Safely in the lift, Nigel turned back.

"Thank you for playing waitress this afternoon Julie", he said.

Julie kissed him on the cheek.

"Mark and I will see you at dinner", she said. "Have you decided what to do about Mr Cape".

"I think so ..... yes I think so", said Nigel.

He pushed the button marked "First floor".

The doors closed.

Julie went back to the sun lounge. In a high backed chair, on the opposite side of the room, a young man was waiting for her. He held a baby in his arms. His daughter. Julie took the child. Captain Mark Rossi smiled with relief. They didn't train you for baby care in the SAS. They really should have done, he thought. They really should .... after all .... Handsome young officer. Stunningly attractive young female linguist .... it could only have one result. Ah well, he thought:

He who Dares, Wins !

THIRTY

We came out of the garden onto the road that led up to Golgotha. We were barely two hundred metres from the city walls. Phillip pointed to a crowd of people moving slowly in our direction.

I remember the colours. I'd been astonished by the brightness of the Magdalena's clothing .... and here again, I was surprised by the variety and brightness of the colours amongst the crowd that were heading towards us.

And I remember the horror of it all. Although I'd read enough about the Roman method of execution called crucifixion .... two thousand years tend to soften the edges.

As the leading soldiers came to within fifty metres of us, we caught our first glimpse of the condemned men. I heard Doctor Samuels draw in her breath sharply. Mark, on my right, said something .... I didn't catch it. I saw Julie grip his hand tightly.

None of the victims were carrying their crosses. The first two were obviously barely capable of supporting themselves, and were being part carried, part dragged, along the road, by the Roman soldiers detailed to execute them.

The first struggled between his captors. He was screaming and sobbing. His tears fell from raw holes. The terrible bruising on his cheeks and brow told the story. The lead tipped flagrum had caught him full across the face, and torn his eyes from their sockets. He was naked, his body streaked with dried blood. Behind him came two women carrying the cross bar for his crucifixion.

Mark turned to me.

"I don't think I was prepared for this", he said.

I shook my head. Doctor Samuels asked if I was Ok.

I nodded. I didn't trust myself to speak.

The second man, also supported by two Roman soldiers, appeared, at first sight, to be in slightly better shape.

Until he had passed us.

Only then did we see that his back, his buttocks, and the upper part of his legs, were torn to ribbons of raw flesh. Streams of fresh blood ran down his calves. He had somehow managed to retain his sandals. They were soaked red crimson .... glued to his feet.

Julie sobbed.

"I can't watch this", she said.

"They used the sheep bone flagrum on that one", said Doctor Samuels. "He's lost a lot of blood already .... he can't survive long on the cross".

I looked at her.

"Yes", she said. "I've seen worse injuries .... but it's the cruelty here that's sickening".

And finally we saw the man we had come to save.

He was the only one of the three who was walking unaided .... but it was obvious that He was near the end of his strength. He had the tattered remains of a garment around His waist. His bare torso was a mass of purple bruising. He had a swelling over His right eye. And strangely .... and yet we should have expected it .... His head was encircled by a woven mass of thorns. Streams of dried blood caked His face. Wounds from the thorn spikes.

"I was right", said Doctor Samuels. "He hasn't been flogged quite as brutally as the others. They are hoping to keep Him alive on the cross for longer. To make a spectacle .... an example of Him".

I looked at Mark. Were we really just going to stand there and watch this happen.

Mark took Julie's hand firmly .... and led us out into the passing crowd. We kept our heads down.

"I'm trying to spot The Magdalena", he said.

I couldn't sense Her presence at all.

"Nigel", said Doctor Samuels, "I need you to do your stuff. I need to know what mental state He's in".

I looked back at her and nodded.

We walked on, suiting our pace to that of the stumbling condemned men.

I took a deep breath .... and opened the door in my mind. I immediately realised that there were others in that crowd who could do the same. I picked up their mood of tension .... and hoplessness.

But as for Jesus of Nazareth .... nothing. He had blocked me out. He knew I was there .... but He had blocked me out. Nothing doing.

It took me by surprise. I felt helpless.

The Doctor was watching me closely.

I shook my head.

"Just keep trying", she said. "He has His reasons, I think".

The dreadful march continued. The first of the victims screamed and sobbed. The following crowd was strangely silent.

We began to climb the final steeper part of the path to the hill top. The Centurion shouted some orders.

The crowd came slowly out onto the plateau of barren rock.

I noticed that the bodies we had seen yesterday were gone. But the crosses were still there, laying in readiness, on the ground.

Mark looked at us.

"Are you all up for this", he said.

I shrugged my shoulders. Julie shook her head, and turned away. Doctor Samuels caught her arm, and spoke softly to her. She stood, head bowed, listening.

"Here we go", said Mark. "It's showtime".

The blinded man was pulled towards an upright laying on the ground. The women brought the cross bar. The Centurion detailed two men to lash it into a rebate in the upright. The man was pulled down until his back lay on the cross. The soldiers took his arms, and pulled them along the cross bar. They lashed the wrists in place .... then stood aside as the Centurion came up, holding a hammer, and two iron spikes.

The blinded man began to scream again, straining at the lashings on his wrists. The Centurion knelt, placed the first nail carefully centred on the lashing, and in two swift blows, drove it through the condemned man's wrist into the crossbar. There was a strong spurt of blood, much of it ending on the Centurions tunic. He appeared not to notice.

"He's hit an artery", said the Doctor. "That's not meant to happen".

Ignoring the blood pouring from the wound, the Centurion went to the other arm, and drove the second spike through the wrist. There was no spurt of blood this time .... but the victim screamed.

I turned away. I retched violently. The Doctor put her arm around my shoulders.

If you think you've heard somebody scream .... I can tell you that you haven't .... not till you've seen a Roman crucifixion.

The Doctor pulled me round.

They pushed the mans legs up, holding his heels on either side of the vertical post. The Centurion produced two more nails, and drove them through the sides of his feet, into the upright.

Three soldiers went to the head of the cross. They lifted it, and a fourth guided the foot of the upright into a slot cut into the stone. They pushed the cross up, then secured it at the base, driving the tapered wooden wedges firmly into place.

The crucified man strained on the spikes, his chest convulsed. His bowel evacuated in a heated, stinking, blood streaked stream. He sagged .... his head sinking onto his chest.

"He's dead", said the Doctor. "Major trauma leading to heart failure, I should think".

The second victim had been held close by, so that he could enjoy a full view of the first execution. The Centurion turned towards him. He began to struggle in panic. One of the soldiers hit him a glancing blow on the head with a baton, then hit him again, fully on the mouth, smashing his teeth through his lips. As they forced him down onto the cross, he coughed a gout of blood, saliva, and fragments of teeth, over his persecutors. They laughed .... the man screaming in terror, as they drove the spikes through his wrists and ankles.

They pushed the cross upright, leaving it just a little short of vertical, before wedging it into place. The victim hung on the nails. He pushed upwards with his legs, trying to breathe, then vomited violently. He hung sobbing, the sound seeming to emanate from deep in his chest. A stream of excrement ran down the cross and pooled on the ground.

Mark turned to me. His face was ashen.

"Fuck this for a game of soldiers", he said. "There's no way they're doing that to Jesus".

It was the first time I'd ever heard him swear.

We've got to be quick", he said. "Are you with me to stop this".

"What the hell are you going to do", I said.

He reached into his tunic, and produced two modern handguns. I recognised the type immediately. They were Walther P38 automatic pistols. Mark pushed off the safety catches, and handed me one.

"We've got to be quick", he said

"Are you crazy", I said. "What about history".

"Fuck history", he said.

He turned, and shot the centurion, point blank through the side of his head. Mark didn't give any quarter. We'd hired an SAS man. That's what we were getting.

The remaining soldiers were frozen in disbelief. Their commanding officer was on the ground with the whole side of his head missing. Mark gave them no chance. Three more went down to headshots. It was too late to think of history now.

"Take your two with chest shots Nigel", he shouted at me.

I shot the man who'd been smashing teeth a few moments earlier. His companion was brave enough to draw his sword. I shot him twice in the chest, hoping for the heart.

By now the whole area was screaming chaos. People were running in all directions .... but with one single thing in mind. To get as far away from this crazed place of execution as possible.

"Mark", I screamed.

The last of the Roman soldiers was drawing back his spear arm to launch the pilum straight at Mark's back".

Mark span round, raised his pistol, and shot the man in the forehead. The pilum clattered to the ground.

Then, seemingly without drawing breath, Mark walked over, picked up the spear, crossed himself in best Roman Catholic tradition, and plunged the spear point into the crucified man's side.

Peace descended upon Golgotha.

We stood there, and looked about us. The crowd had gone. Our only company was a young man wearing a crown of thorns .... and a young woman kneeling at His feet. It was Mary Magdalene. She looked up at us and smiled.

"Mark", I said, "Have you any idea what you've just done".

"I've saved the greatest teacher who ever lived .... that's what I've just done", said Mark. "Bollocks to history .... it's over rated anyway".

Doctor Samuels looked around her. For a lady who had just seen seven men killed in barely as many seconds .... she seemed remarkably calm.

"There was really no need for the spear", she said. "He was already dead".

Julie ran to Mark, and threw herself into his arms. She was crying hysterically. Marked stroked her hair, trying to calm her.

The Magdalena had her arms around Jesus' legs. He bent and stroked her hair.

Doctor Samuels and I looked at each other. I threw my arms open. She laughed. We embraced.

"I still have a patient", she said. "I think I should tend to His wounds".

We walked over to Jesus and The Magdalena. She stood. Mark and Julie joined us.

The Magdalena took each of us in turn, and introduced us to Jesus. He stepped forward to each of us, and placed His palm on our foreheads.

I had always imagined that I would kneel before this man when I met Him. But I didn't. I looked at Him, and remembered that, last night, He had washed His Disciples feet. It was understanding He sought .... not just adoration.

He looked at me .... and opened the door. Just for a moment.

Am I going to describe to you what that felt like.

No way .... you can find your own Jesus.

* * *

Doctor Samuels examined her patient. Having satisfied herself that He was not in immediate danger of collapse, she asked Julie to explain to Him that He should come with us to the tomb in the garden nearby, where she had treatments for the cuts and bruises. In the meantime She gave Him a bottle of rehydration fluid. Julie explained that He must sip it steadily.

Mark took the Doctor aside. They conversed. I saw her look at Jesus with some concern. Eventually she nodded. They seemed to have reached some agreement.

Mark came back to us.

"Ok" he said, "I want us all out of here ASAP. We are marching straight back to our transport outside Bethany. The Roman army are going to want to talk to somebody about this mess .... and we don't want it to be us".

"We're going to have a lot of explaining to do to somebody", I said.

"Later Nigel", said Mark. "Lets march".

"Our gear at the tomb....", I asked.

"Nothing there of much consequence", said Mark. "A suit of Roman armour, tea making gear, and some treatments the Doctor brought. We can trust Phillip to clear it up".

Julie, speaking to The Magdalena in Aramaic, explained what was happening , glancing at Jesus as she did so, to see if He was following. She seemed shy of speaking to Him directly. Jesus, perceiving this, took her hand and spoke to her. She blushed, and bobbed a curtsey.

It was a pretty moment. Jesus smiled at her.

"Is somebody going to take those wretched thorns off His head", said Mark.

He plucked the crown from Jesus' head .... was about to toss it aside .... then changed his mind.

"Nigel", he said. "Give me a hand ".

He went to the unused third cross, and started to drag the upright over to the second crucifixion. Seeing what he had in mind, I helped him lift it, until we had it propped against the rear of the standing cross.

"Hold it steady for me Nigel", he said.

He shinned up .... and placed the crown of thorns firmly on the dead man's head.

He came down, and we threw the upright aside.

I raised my eyebrows at him.

"You work it out", he said.

He thought for a moment.

"Have a look about, and see if you can you see a sign with "King of the Jews" written on it", he said.

We cast about. If it was there .... well .... we couldn't find it.

"I always had my doubts about that sign", said the Doctor.

The others came over. They looked up at the crucified man.

"And they looked upon him whom they pierced", said Doctor Samuels.

"Amen", I said.

*   *   *

Mark got his platoon into marching formation. He broke the head from the spear, and handed the resulting staff to Jesus. He tucked the spear point into his own belt.

"Present for Chris Haines", he said.

He looked at Jesus.

"Nigel", he said. "We are going to have to cover the injuries to His back. Can you spare your outer coat".

I took the coat off, and The Magdalena and I wrapped it carefully around Jesus' shoulders. I could hardly bring myself to look at the damage. The flesh was pulverised. There were purple swellings down His spine. In places the skin was torn open, and stood out as hardened ridges from the clots of dried blood.

It had only been his tormentors intention to keep Him alive on the cross, that had saved Him from even worse.

Mark took a final glance around. He nodded.

"Lets go", he said.

It wasn't going to be a speedy trip.

The sudden release from danger, the presence of Mary Magdalene, and the rehydration drink from the Doctor, had all done much to restore Jesus' energy.

But we had to remember .... He was still badly injured from the flogging.

Mark kept us going steadily. He and I walked on either side of Jesus, ready to support Him if neccessary.

We stopped just once to rest.

Mark astounded us by producing cans of "Red Bull" from somewhere. He flipped the top of the first can, and handed it to The Magdalena. She drank from it, and passed it to Jesus. He examined the can carefully .... but encouraged by The Magdalena .... He drank .... and grimaced.

I smiled. I did the same, the first time I tried it.

So we sat beneath an olive tree on the side of the road, and drank from our cans.

I suddenly saw the scene as one of those classic Victorian religious paintings: "Jesus rests on the road to Bethany".

I wondered what "Red Bull" would pay for the rights to the image.

THIRTY ONE

We didn't meet many people on the road. A few late comers for the Passover holiday. Julie greeted them as they passed us. Some of them exchanged a few words with her.

It was nearly noon by the time we reached our destination.

The Doctor had kept a close eye on her patient. The Magdalena had talked quietly to Him for most of the journey .... no doubt explaining who we were .... and what was happening.

We came to a halt. Mark looked up and down the road. There was nobody in sight.

"I'll just have a quick look at things", he said.

He ran up the slope, stood there for a moment, then burst out laughing.

We exchanged puzzled glances.

Mark came back down,

"What were you laughing at", I said.

"The goat", he said.

"What goat", Julie asked.

"When I looked down at the platform we built", Mark said, "there was a goat standing in the middle of it. It looked up at me .... bleated once .... then disappeared into thin air. It must have caught the twelve o'clock transfer".

He laughed again.

"It was the expression on it's face just before it disappeared", he said. "You had to see it ....".

"That means we'll be waiting for the one o'clock trip home then", I said.

"Guess so", said Mark, still laughing, "It also means that John and Peter have just acquired a goat".

He started to laugh again. He collapsed onto the ground, and laughed, and laughed. He lay on his back, and looked up at us.

"I'm sorry", he said. "It's the thought of John and Peter chasing a first century goat around their smart workspace. Did you ever see that episode of "Blue Peter" with the baby elephant".

We had seen it. We laughed. It was infectious. We laughed until we collapsed to the ground next to him.

The Magdalena looked at us. She looked to Jesus, and shrugged Her shoulders helplessly. He smiled at Her. He understood.

Eventually we recovered our composure.

"Can you apologise to The Magdalena for us Julie", said Mark.

We climbed the rise, and descended to our carefully marked platform. Instead of the earth and stones we had built up .... there was now a neatly levelled surface of clean building sand .... transferred from Peter and John's end of things.

I was reminded of something .... something recently ....

Mark nodded approvingly, and checked his watch.

"Thirty five minutes to wait", he said. "But we'll get on board ten minutes early. I don't see why we shouldn't all go together. Plenty of room if we all stand".

Marks gear was where he had left it. The goat had chewed the straps on one pack, but it hadn't managed to break in. Mark handed us bottles of water. It was warm .... but we sat under the tree, and sipped it gratefully.

Doctor Samuels took the opportunity to examine Jesus' back.

"I'm worried about infection", she said. "The sooner I can clean and sterilise these wounds, the happier I'll be".

She helped her patient put his coat back on.

"Tell Him not to worry", she said to Julie. "We're nearly home".

I must have dozed off for a moment. Mark was shaking me.

"Time to go", he said.

We assembled on the sand platform. There was plenty of room, but Mark asked us to crouch down a little.

"I want plenty of headroom", he said.

He brought out his watch.

"Final minute", he said.

At thirty seconds he began a countdown.

"Fingers and toes tucked in", said the Doctor, as he reached the count of ten.

"Five .... four .... three .... two .... one .... go", said Mark.

There was no drama. We were there .... and then we were back. Simple as that.

Mark looked at Peter, who was standing there waiting.

"What did you do with the goat", he asked.

*   *   *

John, on the other side of the room, looked up from his computer screen.

"It's probably best if you all come out of the cube", he said.

He and Peter had placed chairs, and a table, for us .... well away from the "transporter". The table had a collection of canned drinks on it.

"You don't know how pleased we are to see you all", said Peter.

"Well you asked us to "get Him out", said Mark. "Here He is ".

John stepped forward to meet the man known as Jesus of Nazareth.

"I'm John", he said . He offered his hand. Jesus took it.

Peter came and stood next to John.

"And I'm Peter", he said.

Jesus looked thoughtfully at Peter. He spoke .... in Aramaic.

Peter looked to Julie.

"He wants you to build a Church for Him", said Julie.

"Nobody is building anything for the moment", Doctor Samuels said. "I need to examine this young man and cleanse His wounds".

She crossed the room and opened the doors on to what appeared to be a well equipped medical area. In the centre was an examination table, with a smoothed white sheet on it.

"Julie", she said .... if you will".

Julie shepherded Jesus, and The Magdalena, through the doors. She smiled back at us, stepped through herself, and closed the doors behind her.

Mark and I were left alone with John and Peter.

John looked at us questioningly.

"Did you have any problems then", he said.

I took a deep breath .... and looked to Mark.

"How's the goat", said Mark.

Peter laughed. He walked over to the window, and pulled up the blind. There, tethered, on a piece of untidy ground behind the building, was the goat. It had already done a lot of damage to the bushes. It was chewing on a piece of white polystyrene packaging. It stopped to look at us. It was obviously well content.

I suppose, for a goat, having interesting things to chew on is pretty much your goal in life .... that, and making more goats. It continued chewing happily on the packaging.

"I'll sort it out with a bucket of water later", said Peter.

We turned back into the room. We sat at the table with Peter and John. We cracked the tops on cans of Coke.

"There are no wounds in His feet", said John.

"Or his wrists", said Peter.

"No there aren't ", said Mark.

There was a long silence. We sipped our Cokes.

"Do you want to tell us", said John.

Mark looked at them both. We waited. Mark put down his Coke.

"We've got a lot to discuss", he said, "And I need to do some thinking. Let's sort it out over dinner".

John nodded.

"Ok", he said, "I'll let Simon know you're back".

Mark stood.

"Does that room we changed in yesterday have a bathroom", he asked.

"Yes .... it's ensuite". said Peter.

"Great", said Mark, "I'm off for a shower. I was up half the night .... so I want to get some sleep. What do you want to do Nigel".

"Pretty much the same", I said.

"Give me ten minutes start then", he said.

He left the room.

Peter looked at me.

"Nigel", he said. "What have you done".

I thought for a moment.

"Peter", I said. "Do you have a Bible here".

"I think we do", he said.

He went to a filing cabinet, and opened the top drawer.

"Yes", he said.

He handed me the Bible.

I checked the front pages. It was a revised King James version. That would do. I turned to each of the four Gospels in turn, Mathew, Mark, Luke, and John. I read the final verses of each. I closed the book, looked at Peter, and smiled.

"We're good", I said.

Peter went to speak, but I shook my head.

I headed for the shower.

THIRTY TWO

There was a knock on the door. I woke, and pulled myself up in the bed. Across the room, in the half light, I saw Mark stirring as well. I switched on the bedside light.

"Are you decent Mark", I asked.

"Always", he said. He stretched, and sat up.

"Come in", I called.

It was Doctor Samuels. She came in, leaving the door slightly ajar. She had changed back into modern clothing. She stood smiling at us.

"My .... don't you two look cosy", she said.

"Flashdance .... 1983", I said.

"Pardon", she said.

"It's a line from the film "Flashdance", I said. "The bit where the ex-wife finds Alex and Nick in the posh restaurant".

"How do you remember stuff like that", she said.

"Haven't got a clue", I said.

"How's the patient", said Mark.

"He's doing just fine", she said. "We got Him cleaned up. Two of the flogging wounds are right down to the bone, but I've cleaned them out, and there's no sign of infection yet, but I've got some antibiotics into Him anyway. He did start to show some signs of delayed shock ....".

"I suffer that way", I said.

".... so I've given Him a mild sedative. He'll sleep for ten hours or so".

"How's Julie", said Mark.

Doctor Samuels smiled.

"She's Ok", she said. "Poor girl had to go and throw up once .... but I've got to hand it to her .... she came right back .... and got on with the job".

"And The Magdalena", I asked.

"Serene as always", said the Doctor. "I've sent them both off to bed. We're going to take turns at watching Him tonight".

"How long did we sleep", I asked.

"It's six o'clock now", she said.

"What's the plan for the evening", said Mark.

"Simon is going to bring a takeaway here for about seven thirty .... Indian, I think. We'll fix up a table next to the cube. We won't be far from the medical room, if we're needed.

Mark nodded.

"Sounds good", he said.

"I'll leave you to get dressed", said the Doctor.

She went out, closing the door behind her.

I lay back on the pillows.

"Mark", I said. "How did you know I would be able to use that Walther".

"Chris Haines told me", he said.

"Ah", I said.

"Did we bring the guns back with us", I said.

"We certainly did", said Mark. "We don't want anybody altering history with a firearm that hasn't been invented yet".

"Unless it's you....", I said.

He laughed.

"I need the loo", he said.

He got up, and disappeared into the bathroom. I got out of bed, and dressed in trousers, and a shirt. It felt strange after the first century garb.

* * *

Mark came back in. He dressed, then looked at me thoughtfully.

"There's tea making gear on that side table", he said. "Is there any water in the kettle".

I looked.

"I'll fill it in the bathroom", I said.

* * *

We sat in the two chairs and sipped our tea.

"How are you feeling about your part in things this morning", Mark asked me.

"Not too good", I said.

"Never shot anyone before", he said.

"No .... never", I said. "How about you ....".

"Unfortunately yes", he said. "Comes with the job".

I looked at him .... and lowered my head. I wasn't good with it .... not good at all.

"Stand up", said Mark sharply.

I stood .... surprised by his tone.

He came over and put his arms round me.

"You did your part well", he said. "They were fully trained professional soldiers. The only thing we had going for us was the element of surprise .... and even then.... if you hadn't warned me about the one with the spear ....".

I looked at him. I started to cry.

He let me.

*   *   *

By a quarter to seven everybody was in the main room. Simon had brought over the plates, and the glasses, and the cutlery .... even a table cloth .... and set things up in a very civilised manner. He'd gone off to get the takeaway.

By leaving the medical room door open, Doctor Samuels could keep an eye on her patient. I looked in at Him. He was fast asleep.

Simon appeared with carrier bags filled with lots of containers. Six different mains, various rices, mixed vegetables, four different naan breads, and, of course, the poppudums .... with the dips.

As he wasn't cooking .... Simon joined us at the table, and for the next few minutes, it was the normal Indian takeaway chaos, as we shared it all out.

We ate. We ate until we ran out of steam .... and then we ate poppudums .... until we ran out of those too.

Eventually we pushed back our chairs, and surveyed the debris in the middle of the table.

"I'll clear it in a moment", said Simon.

"No hurry Simon", said John. "Lets hear what Mark has to tell us first".

All eyes turned to Mark.

"Captain Rossi", said John. "Debrief if you please .... you have the floor".

Mark had training and experience on his side. That was obvious. For the next fifteen minutes he gave us a clear and concise account of the operation, from beginning to end. From our arrival in the Holy Land .... to our return with the mission successfully completed.

"So in conclusion", said Mark, "I think the whole thing went really well. Subject secured. All team members safely back".

There was a long silence. Peter looked to John. John sat there looking at us all, as though unable to know where to start.

"You've altered history", he said eventually.

"Doubt it", said Mark.

"But....", said Peter.

"Have you got a Bible here", said Mark.

"Ahead of you on that one", I said. "I checked already .... there are no differences. None at all".

Mark smiled. I did think that he looked just a little relieved .... but he concealed it well.

"I don't follow you", said John

"Nigel knows the four Gospels really well", Mark said. "If we did alter history, then the Bible you have here would be different .... particularly as regards the crucifixion. Nigel says it's the same. We didn't alter anything. And .... to be honest .... I didn't think we would".

John stared at him.

"Tell us why", he said.

"Ok", said Mark. "Take the word "history". You all know that I studied "history". But what did I really study. Did I study what really happened in the past .... or did I study what somebody else had written about what happened in the past. There is only one possible way to know what really happened .... now .... or in the past. You have to watch it happen with your own eyes. The five of us that you sent back to Jerusalem .... we know exactly what happened at Golgotha this morning. We were there to see it".

"But how do you explain the descriptions in the Gospels", said Peter.

"In history", said Mark. "That is to say, real history .... as in things that really happened .... there are winners .... and there are losers. Usually the winners get to write the story of what happened .... and .... amazingly .... they write it to suit themselves. To suit their own future".

"So who won this morning", said John.

"The Church won", said Mark. "They always do. It will be thirty years before Paul writes anything .... and he certainly wasn't at Golgotha this morning .... and it will be fifty years or more until the first of the Gospels is written. And only Mark's Gospel can .... by anybody experienced in reading statements .... be taken as eye witness.

Written history is always one simple thing. It's what the winners want to happen .... and what the Church will want to happen then .... and what they still want now .... is a dead Jesus. A dead person is much more convenient for writers of biographies, because that dead person isn't in a position to argue about what you've written about them.

As we sit here, there are just eight people who know what really happened at the crucifixion at Golgotha. But nobody would believe a word of it, because of those four accounts in the Gospels. As I said. We didn't alter a single thing".

"The Qur'an", has Jesus escaping the cross", said Peter.

"And the people of India tell us that Jesus returned there, lived to about eighty years old, and is buried in a tomb in Kashmir", said Mark, "Does anybody take them seriously .... No".

"So where does that leave the Christian faith", said John.

"Same as ever", said Mark. "They needed a dead Jesus .... and a dead Jesus is what they wrote for themselves. His death means their sins are forgiven .... wiped clean. They are "washed in the blood of the lamb". It's an attractive concept .... of course they needed a dead Jesus. Much easier than studying His teachings, and trying to live according to His code. Imagine living your life like that. Much too much like hard work. No .... Jesus died to save me from my sins .... job done. Jesus did it for me. Game over. Easy life".

"I'm a Christian", said John.

Mark turned to him. He was on fire ....

"Are you really, John", he said. "Are you really a Christian. Do you think I didn't notice that sand on the floor in the tomb. What were you going to do John .... put Him back there. What was the plan John ....

So you're a Christian are you. Well let's put that to the test shall we. And we'll do it in one simple question.

Jesus of Nazareth is laying in that room there .... I rescued Him. But what do you think, John. Perhaps you'd rather He was brutally tortured and murdered .... in the way we saw this morning .... so you can have your sins forgiven .... or would you rather we save Him, so that He can continue His teaching .... so that He can spread Love and Compassion, and Tolerance and Understanding, in a world that's seriously lacking in all of those things".

John stared down at his plate

"Come through those doors with me, John", Mark said. "I'll show you the wounds on His back .... and while you're looking at those .... I'll tell you what really happens when they drive the nails through the wrists and the feet. Come through those doors with me. I'll show you the greatest teacher who ever lived. So will you come and listen to his teachings ..... or would you rather I'd left Him nailed to that cross .... so you can tell everybody, "He died for my sins".

John stared at him.

"Come on then John", said Mark. "You said you were a Christian .... I want a proper Christian answer .... and I want it now.

Which is it to be John".

The question hung in the air .... nailed to a cross.

John rose from the table. He placed his chair neatly back beneath it. He walked over to the medical room doors, and pushed them open. He stood .... looking down at the young man asleep on the table. Then he bent forwards, and kissed Him on the forehead.

He stood there a few moments more, then left us .... passing the table on his way to the door.

And not one of us had the courage to look at him.

THIRTY THREE

Editor's notes.

You have just finished reading the "unpublished" first edition of "get Him out "…..with the obvious additions of chapters twenty eight, and twenty nine.

As Nigel White said to me:

"I wrote thirty chapters, to reach one simple question".

* * *

It's normal to conclude a book of this nature by telling you what happened to the team members. I have their permission to do so:

Captain Mark Rossi served the remaining months of his time with the SAS. He married Miss Julie Parker Smith, and they went to live in the Languedoc area of France. They took a set of "Tribbles", and a goat, with them.

Doctor Verena Samuels became director of the Medical Center she built with John Forbes. They both campaign for the abolition of Capital Punishment , in those countries where it is still practised. Their organisation has a motto:

"Vengeance is Mine, sayeth the Lord".

Simon became Director of Catering for Premier Travel Inns. He married John Forbes' daughter, Tara, five years ago, and now works as an assistant to John, and Doctor Verena Samuels.

Peter White did build a church. Above the altar hangs the image of Jesus of Nazareth. There are no wounds in His hands. There are no wounds in His feet. There is no cross in the Church. I went to a Sunday morning service there recently.

The lesson was "The woman taken in Adultery".

Nigel White retired from business. He decided on a long holiday in the lake district .... at the Langdon Chase Hotel.

During his first week there, he was woken one night by agonising pains in his wrists and feet. The pains continue to this day. There is no medical explanation for them. He still lives at The Langdon Chase Hotel.

The Magdalena went back to the first century .... but to southern France, where She was welcomed by friends of Joseph of Arimathea. Her child was born there. She was just eighteen years old.

After a year there .... she missed the "connection" she had shared with Nigel , and returned to spend her time in the world that she had found so fascinating .... a world that had ice cream. She brought her daughter, Madeleine, with her.

Jesus of Nazareth disappeared from John and Peter's facility that night. He had used the "cube" to return to His own time and place. Whether John had left the apparatus"switched on", or whether Jesus Himself had managed to give it life, will never be known. Before He left .... Jesus had knelt and written in the sand.

The language was Aramaic.

Julie translated it as:

"Where I am going .... you cannot follow".

Editor: Jonathan Cape

THIRTY FOUR

Far away .... in Jerusalem .... Joseph of Arimathea sought a body from Pontious Pilate.

Pilate marvelled that He be dead so soon. He looked to the man in the uniform of a Centurion, standing next to Joseph. Pilate looked again. He didn't recognise this Centurion. Ah well .... these young officers .... they came and went so fast .... it was difficult to keep up with them.

Pilate granted the body. He watched them depart. He stirred uneasily in his chair. He wished he had handled the whole business differently.

At Golgotha, Joseph, Nicodemus, and Phillip, removed the body from the cross. Joseph looked sadly at the young man laying there dead.

They carried him to the tomb. They treated his body with herbs and spices .... as is the custom of the Jews at burial. And they laid him in a shroud .... a length of Fabric that Joseph had bought for the purpose. It had been in the parcel that he had sent up to the tomb the previous evening.

As they wrapped the body, by the light of two small lamps, Joseph looked again, at the material. It seemed whiter than he remembered it. He examined it more closely. It was very fine linen, with a strange weave. He drew Nicodemus' attention to the cloth. Nicodemus shrugged. Wrapping a dead body, by lamplight, in a dimly lit tomb, late in the evening, was not his idea of pleasure.

There were places he would rather be.

The three men finished their work. Joseph led them in a prayer for the departed. They went out .... and rolled the door across the entrance. They filled in the trench behind the door stone. The tomb was sealed.

* * *

High on the mountain path .... the air had cooled a little. The scorching heat of the afternoon sun had abated, and the two men prepared to resume their journeys. It had taken them nearly two years to reach this point .... the point where their ways lay in different directions. The older of the two must go south .... into the heart of the continent. He had a message to deliver.

The younger man would turn to the east. He was within three days journey of the Monastery that had educated him. He had made a promise to return. He wondered if any of his teachers still lived.

The two men stood .... knowing that the moment to part had finally arrived .... and then they embraced. They had talked for two years .... and now there was nothing left to say.

The younger man kissed the older on the forehead. Then he turned to the east, and walked away. The older man shouldered his pack .... and watched his companion, until he was out of sight. He raised his arm to call a final farewell .... then lowered it ....

He smiled. They would meet again ....

* * *

"Nigel", said Mark, looking over my shoulder. "There are some capital letters missing in that piece".

"Are you sure about that Mark", I said.

THE END

AND FINALLY

There is one person who is not in this book .... and that is not fair, because he gave me his support from the beginning.

He gave me his support .... when he might have hesitated.

And he gave me his support when I least expected it .... when others had faltered.

There are reasons why I cannot put him in this book .... but his support has been in my mind throughout.

He may feel that this book is a step too far .... but I hope he will understand why I have written it.

SUGGESTED READING

The Passover Plot, Hugh Schonfield. 1965

The Holy Blood and the Holy Grail, Michael Baigent, Richard Leigh and Henry Lincoln. 1982

The Case for the Real Jesus, Lee Strobel. 2007

The Shroud, Ian Wilson. 2010

The Gospel of Thomas, Judas Thomas. Unknown

The New Testament, Various authors. Unknown

SUGGESTED LISTENING

This is our God, Hillsong

Forever (Live), Kari Jobe

Rooftops, Jesus Culture

Days of Elijah, Judy Jacobs

Great are You Lord, Sinach

Also By Nigel White

".... watching people cry"

A sequel to "get Him out".

Debbie and Roger are an unlikely couple. A very unlikely couple indeed, and by all that's right and sensible, they should never have met at all ....

Because Miss Deborah Anne Wintersham is the poshest of posh society girls .... and Mr Roger Davies is a car dealer. A car dealer who goes to Church ....

Roger knows a lot about cars .... he knows even more about girls. And he knows that Awesome God loves an honest car dealer.

But Debbie, is not quite what she seems. The world she comes from is very different. And from the moment they meet, the surprises come thick and fast, both for Roger .... and for his "minder", Uncle John.

Debbie introduces John to her "Very bestest of best friends", Lorraine, and the two couples are soon planning a double wedding.

But Roger's world is one of conflict and intolerance. Two young men from another culture are preparing to glorify themselves in the eyes of their God.

Fresh from a hair dressing appointment, at their favourite Salon, Debbie, and Lorraine find themselves in the wrong place .... at the wrong time.

Roger, John, and those around them, must try to come to terms with what has happened. But Roger refuses to surrender ....

And then the recurrent dreams begin. A duffle coat on the rear seat of a car.

Eventually realising the dream's significance, Roger makes a phone call .... and is offered an incredible opportunity. An opportunity to meet the one man in all of Human history who can restore what Roger has lost.

What has happened to Roger has changed his life forever .... but this plea for help will leave him standing in a doorway between two worlds, with a decision to make that could change history. For himself .... for those closest to him .... and for those who have made his dreams come true.

".... watching people cry", is a roller coaster ride. A ride from the sublime joy of new romance .... to the darkest despair of love lost .... to a finale that will leave you questioning your relationship with the world you inhabit.